SEASON
to
TASTE

SEASON
to
TASTE

A Novel

NATALIE YOUNG

Little, Brown and Company
New York Boston London

Copyright © 2014 by Natalie Young

Little, Brown and Company
Hachette Book Group
237 Park Avenue, New York, NY 10017
littlebrown.com

First North American Edition: July 2014

Originally published in Great Britain by Tinder Press, an imprint of Headline Publishing Group, January 2014

Little, Brown and Company is a division of Hachette Book Group, Inc. The Little, Brown name and logo are trademarks of Hachette Book Group, Inc.

The publisher is not responsible for websites (or their content) that are not owned by the publisher.

The Hachette Speakers Bureau provides a wide range of authors for speaking events. To find out more, go to hachettespeakersbureau.com or call (866) 376-6591.

Epigraph by Louise Bourgeois is © The Easton Foundation

ISBN 978-0-316-28248-2
LCCN 2014937383

10 9 8 7 6 5 4 3 2 1

RRD-C

Book design by Carin Dow
Printed in the United States of America

For
Jackie Coventry and Mercy Hooper

Sometimes it is necessary to make a confrontation.
                                        Louise Bourgeois

SEASON
to
TASTE

1

Lizzie got into the Volvo and adjusted the seat and the mirror. On the air in the car and from the upholstery she caught the smell of his buttery skin and the tobacco from him; and she kept that smell in all the way to the lake. With the cold outside and the heating on and the dog breathing in the boot, she managed to trap them both in a white steaming fug and she kept her arm moving against the windscreen to clear a view of the road. It was very silly. But opening the window and letting that smell of her husband go seemed a bit silly too.

She crunched to a halt at the lake and looked at the coins—one and two p's—scattered around the handbrake. There was a piece of paper with a shopping list written in pencil.

Sug
Flo
Egg
Butt
LP

A stub of pencil lay on the floor, with a chewed rubber on the end. At Joanna's house in London he'd experimented with drugs. He hadn't told Lizzie what, or how; only that he'd tried things, and had "a ball." "LP" was loo paper. She stared at the writing and wondered what it meant if a person wrote like that: right up in the corner, taking up so little space, and then leaving all that white. She lifted the piece of paper right up to her eye and closed the other one while trying to read through the blur. Then she dropped it in the driver's door pocket and went out into the air.

Lizzie glimpsed her reflection in the lake and pulled her waterproof coat with the thick fleece lining around her neck. An hour went by and she was still out by the tall trees, and Rita, the enormous Ridgeback, was following on behind her. Lizzie heard the lolloping gait and she felt the mud on the dog's paws as if it were clinging to her own boots.

Her mother had said: you have to manage expectations and disappointment. And try not to drink.

"Yes," said Lizzie, behind the wheel, for she was back in the car already, and she was staring through the windscreen, and the dog was in the boot, waiting, stinking, slumped down.

The rubber gloves at the village shop were a pink foreign kind in a cheap bag, not the lined ones for sensitive hands she usually got from the supermarket. Twice

Lizzie went back to the shelf to return them and then she stood with her neck bent and a foot pushed out while she read the newspapers on the floor until the woman with the huge rise of brown hair at the counter turned from her view of the village green and asked if she was going to take the gloves.

Lizzie took handfuls of carrots, garlic, onions, celery and potatoes to the counter. "Including the paper and the gloves," she said, "I only want to spend ten pounds."

She drove home, and parked the car in its usual spot in the lane, a few meters before the house, half in, half out of the ditch. Then she sat at the wheel for a while longer and looked at the little house behind the hedge, at the redbrick chimney wall with its huge crack, and the trees still stripped, still bare and dark and wet with winter.

The agent would say: "Sweet little house. Looks a bit hemmed in. Cozy, though."

Jacob had been dead three days. Now he was in the freezer in sixteen bits. Lizzie would start cooking him this afternoon. She'd known as she bent down to check his pulse on the lawn on Monday that burying him in the woods wasn't an option, and not just because she lacked the muscle, or the nerve, to dig a sizable hole. It was more to do with what came after: thoughts of his body coming up once she'd gone, shifting in the ground during a freak storm, during the sudden uprooting of an old tree and the clearing of leaves in a gully. Then a dog or a walker would find him and that would be the end of it. In the future, a telephone would be ringing, a mobile lighting up on a kitchen table she'd chosen for herself online. She'd be called back from wherever it was she'd run to, brought back to the Surrey woods in a police car, forced to confront, sent down.

Lizzie opened the boot and watched the dog pee on the verge and then slither under the yew hedge to the garden. If she had planned to stay here she might have slipped Jacob's body into the swampy marshland on either side of the lane where nothing went and it was always dark. She'd have tethered him down among the tufts of elephant grass and known he was rotting close to home for a decade.

It would have been all right because no one, not the postman nor the grown-up kids from the farm nor the ramblers gone astray from the South Downs Way, would believe in a rotten old corpse around here. The Surrey Hills, and this part especially, off the A31 between Guildford and Farnham, was a leafy exclusion on the commuter belt where people put up shiny gates and bombed up to London in quiet thrusting cars. At the weekends they made trips to the garden center and had supper parties in the kitchen. They didn't have time to snoop or peer. Even the postman, who came flying over the bumps and puddles, leaving the engine rattling while he hopped up the steps in his jeans and T, was a man juggling work and a start-up and four small children.

She could have done it. She could have slipped Jacob into the swamp and kept him down, said to those in the post office or the village pub, to the woman in the village shop, that her husband had gone to Argentina, or Cambodia, to start a new life with a friend. She wouldn't have needed to say that he'd gone away with a woman from the Pearl in Guildford, for they would have known from the way she paused and hung her head that something delicate had happened.

Lizzie agreed with Jacob's opinion that there were some things missing in her: she wasn't very bright, and it was true that she lacked imagination; but she was practical, and she wasn't going to prison for this. There had been more missing from their thirty-year marriage than was just missing in her, and if one of them was now unfortunately dead, then the one remaining had a chance to move on and live.

Really live, thought Lizzie as she unlocked the front door to her house and carefully pocketed the key.

She would take a train to Scotland. There would be a room in the city of Glasgow with rooftops to look at and a bed and chair. There would be bustle outside, a place to have coffee, and people going about first thing. She would be an early bird, tossing back the covers and up with the worm. She would not be waking to the twittering of birds or the rustle and snap of one more blessed tree. Woodland life had been appealing once, but it had left her with dark bruisy eyes and no friends. It had given her these long bandy legs anxiously lifting up over things.

She would rent a room and work in an office. She would cycle to the library and live frugally and consciously, needing nothing from anyone.

In the porch Lizzie turned and wiped her cheeks. She called softly to the dog crawling back under the yew hedge, and went inside, striding bravely in her jeans through the kitchen, where she put her shopping on the sideboard, and stepped through the interconnecting door to the garage.

She opened up the freezer. His right hand, wrapped in a bin liner and labeled in marker pen, was at the top, in one of the removable wire baskets attached to the rim. It was resting on the bag that contained the left hand. The other parts were underneath the baskets, piled up and labeled in black bags, and mixed in with the frozen vegetables.

Holding on to the rim of the freezer, Lizzie pulled back and stared at the concrete floor. Her mouth was dry. Her watch said eleven thirty-two, which meant she'd lost another hour since her trip to the lake in thin, meandering thought. She listened to the tick of her watch and looked at the ground for blood spots—blood that might have come in on her boots or on the wheel of the wheelbarrow. There hadn't been much. Even out on the grass where she'd bludgeoned him to death.

1. It doesn't matter to anyone—least of all him— which bit you go for. Start with the extremities if that feels more comfortable, but don't be under any illusion about things being easier further from his heart.
2. Take each piece as it comes. Take whatever is there. It is only what it is.
3. Be glad that you're alone to do this. With only the dog to witness what you're doing.
4. IGNORE THE SMELL that will inevitably arise. Bowls of vinegar and bicarbonate of soda can be strategically placed around the house. We'll come on to it later. A clothes peg might be useful for wearing on the nose, with a plaster underneath the peg to prevent skin irritation. If you keep the peg on your nose while eating you will find that it takes the taste of flesh away. Strong coffee, and cinnamon rubbed into the tongue will have the same effect.
5. You can still wear earrings. Some simple turquoise studs might be nice. Or gold? The point is, no one is expecting you to do this with a cloth on your head.

*   *   *

In the kitchen, in the pink gloves, Lizzie took his right hand out of the bag and put the wire twisty back in the drawer. She rinsed the hand in the sink, used the brush to scrub some of the dried blood off, and steamed it clean under the hot tap. She placed a tea towel over the sink, and left the hand to thaw there, out of sight. She put a bowl of vinegar on the window ledge and went to light the fire in the living room. It was where they'd spent most of the marriage, doing the crossword, watching TV. They'd had many rows about money in there, and Jacob had reared up behind the sofa once with that letter-box smile and tried to smother her in the sofa cushions.

"God help us," he'd say, from deep in his throat where his mother was, stuck like a fish bone, tiny and furious.

"You having tea?" he'd say.

"Tea?"

"Cup of tea?"

"I'm sorry, Jacob," she whispered now.

She was still in shock. She sat by the fire in her apron with her knees up and looked at her slippers. She broke a few little white matches in her fingers.

"I'll put the kettle on," he'd say. He'd tried to convert the shed. He'd gone in and out and spent an awful lot of time cleaning the smear from his glasses.

"Tea?"

"Fuck's sake, tea?"

"Tea?"
"You having tea?"

6. Any particularly hateful expressions of his can be jotted down as you go about this. Marriage is rich with pitiful gestures. Expressions, hand movements, mannerisms in general.
7. Don't analyze, or waste time trying to work out why. Write them down as you go past the kitchen table. In time these jottings will become your little army. Be liberal. Watch the lines harden into soldiers and spin upright. Guilt is a vast country that spreads, changing shape. It will grow and attack your borders. Don't let it. Keep your army strong.

Lizzie took the bottle of white from the fridge and poured some into a long-stemmed glass her husband had picked up cheap, in a set of four, from the supermarket. She had decided that the wine would come with the meal, so as to combine first reviving sip with first mouthful of food as part of a reward scheme she was revising in her head, but her pulse was up now, and refraining from a glass at this stage was going to take an act of will she hadn't counted among her challenges this evening. The goal was consumption, and if that meant having a drink before the meal to calm the nerves, or after, to reward herself, she would go with whatever impulse was less significant than the desire to forsake the project entirely. It was a job like any other; the return was in accomplishment, if not the satisfaction, however it was done. A little wine, she felt, was going to be all right.

It wasn't helpful to look at the severed end where the bone emerged with flesh attached and shiny bits of cartilage. So she covered it up with the tea towel and focused on the knuckle area and fingers. She cleaned the nails with a nailbrush, rinsing in the sink; and then she brushed the skin with an oil brush to give it a good crisp. She rubbed all over the hand with olive oil and salt and then twisted the pepper grinder; and she laid his hand on a nonstick roasting tray, carefully straightening the fingers out.

8. Once thawed, each piece will seem a little whiter, maybe a little yellow. That's completely normal. Some blotchiness may have occurred during the chopping up. If it looks a bit purple in places, don't be alarmed.
9. Like rivers of blood, rigor mortis and really terrible blemishing are the stuff of fantasy and television

programs. Actual preparation of a dead body is
practicalities and residing in the mundane.
10. A simple massage once the piece has been defrosted should even out the skin tone.

Out on the patio, in the dark, Lizzie stood in her coat
with the rubber gloves and the apron still on, and she
looked at the trees.

She'd had the oven on its highest setting for half an
hour before she put the hand in. It was much too hot,
but searing the first bit of him beyond recognition
seemed the right way to begin. She had scorched herself
enough times in the garden to know what it was to be
heated at 25 to 30 degrees centigrade. It was immense
dehydration. As with a hangover, but worse. He was in
at 250. His blood would have reached boiling point in
a few minutes. It was much too hot. She should turn it
down a notch. Except there was something to be said for
taking it beyond the look of a human hand. She had no
idea, yet, how she would react to actually having to eat
it. Better, then, to go for the crisp, at this stage: better to
keep it high.

Lizzie shivered. The damp had fully permeated the
little woodcutter's house this week. She'd had several
windows open and candles burning on saucers to take
away the smell. During Monday's dismemberment, the
intestines slipped out onto the lawn like a heap of dead
fish, and the smell that came straight after that, as the

bacteria went into a breeding frenzy, seeped into her nose. The stench followed her around as she did her chores, going up and down the stairs, in and out of the bathroom. She knew that its tenacity, its terrible cling, was to be expected after the horrors on the lawn, and she cleaned the cottage with as much disinfectant as she was able to find in the store cupboard under the stairs, and as many buckets of boiling water as Rita had ever witnessed moving back and forth from her bed on the kitchen floor. Sheets, rugs, blankets and towels: everything was washed, and given an airing; and Lizzie wasn't wearing the peg now—her hair was pinned up and freshly washed—and she wore the tiny pearl earrings. She knew; it was one of the things to watch out for, after getting too drunk on white wine, that the smell was a flight signal direct from her brain: there was death in the house, in the freezer; she should be on that train to Scotland now, looking for a hostel somewhere to bed down.

She breathed, and crossed her arms, lifting her loose breasts under the coat.

It was the beginning of March. By April, certainly, she would be finished, and then her life would be hers. The new life would be structured around avoiding emotional experience at all costs: animated women, news of devastation, kissing couples, feature films, small children, dogs with soupy eyes would be skirted, and walks would be walks for air in the lungs and exercise, not ways of finding a view to alter one's perception of things. Butcher's shops would be dealt with as and when they cropped up, and Lizzie was going to prepare for that. She would be a vegetarian, a fugitive, on the run; holding on to life against all probability, and likely therefore to experience sudden surges of exhilarating relief, though pleasure would be held in check by all that had gone before and the need to keep alert. She would strive for control. Her movements would be measured, interaction minimal.

That was as far as she'd thought about the future—that and leaving Surrey for Scotland. She would use what there was in the house and try not to shop for more until she got there. There wasn't much money in her bank account—there never had been. They owned the house, but she was down to two hundred and forty pounds in her account, and a little more in the joint account. There was a cupboard full of oatcakes, a box of cornflakes, a few tins of soup, some duck fat, vegetables in the box in the garage and in the fridge, four bottles of white wine, and sufficient protein in the freezer to keep her muscles in working order. She would walk the dog, run to keep up an appetite, and to keep her head clear. She would sleep with the help of a little brandy at night, and thereby pursue this chance of a new life.

"Carry on, Lizzie, friend," she'd been whispering to herself since she woke this morning, though she knew it wasn't so much encouragement as an attempt to soothe and soften the tension she could feel on her face. It was there in her jaw; it was in the eyes—enlarged a little and fixed open on the ceiling at night.

It had been a terrible, shocking Monday morning incident. Instead of killing him, she could have taken the dog for a walk, or ventured out in the car to do the shop at the supermarket off the A31. She could have made raisin bread, or looked online. She could have used that desperate feeling to run up the lane with some biscuits and ask Erik and Barbara if they had any work in the house or on the farm. She could have driven to the garden center and waited for them to open so that she could have a wander round inside and look at nice Tom Vickory with his big brown eyes and his face full of feelings. Instead she had chosen to kill her husband on the lawn at 8:15 a.m. with the garden spade. He'd been out in a thin woolen jumper, down by the flower bed, trying to enlarge a hole he'd dug in the autumn for saplings.

Since Monday, then, Lizzie had worn the peg and sniffed menthol and eucalyptus. She had taken to standing in the shed where whiffs of her living husband were still in the air. There were three or four moments of pure denial this week when all senses agreed Jacob was still alive. She smelled him that same afternoon in the shed, and then felt him as a breath at her neck at the kitchen table on Monday and Tuesday night. She even thought she'd seen him, briefly, in the garden, first thing on Wednesday morning, crouching over his hole.

Lizzie knew these were phantoms, but the trickery was enough, so far, to keep her from the paralysis of shock. She had gone up to the bedroom, once, on Tuesday afternoon, to pack a bag. She'd gone to the mirror and saw a tired woman of fifty-three, but her face bore no obvious trace of what she had done. Instead she saw a woman looking headstrong for once in a wispy enclosure of light hair. There was nothing to admire in the mirror, there was absolutely nothing to like; but the face was a face like any other, and altering her perception of it out of self-pity was an indulgence she'd never pursued either. The body of her husband would be consumed, the house cleaned and rented out, and life continued, without sensibility, in Scotland.

2

Actually she hadn't bludgeoned him to death. She'd hit him once on the top of the head. Then she'd swung the spade with both arms from the side and hit him on the back of his head so that his brain shot forward in his skull.

He went down on the grass, falling stiffly like a toy soldier. Lizzie watched his body thud. Then she walked across the grass to get the axe from the back of the shed door. It was easy. She went back into the house and took the rubber gloves and the bin liners from the cupboard under the sink. She fed the dog, and remembered the white twisty ties in the drawer of miscellaneous items. She shut the drawer carefully, and walked backwards through the kitchen, into the garage, then closed the garage door behind her and locked it. It was very quiet out in the frosty garden. The spade and the axe, which were to be her tools, were lying out there beside him, as if put down for her by an imaginary friend, and the landline phone and the mobile on which she might have called the police were locked inside, on the table in the hall.

* * *

For the first cut she'd kept herself very still and focused. With her fingers she made a gap between his sock and jeans. The axe whistled through the air as she brought it down on the bit of white above his sock and she heard it clunk against the bone. She gave it another go, drawing the axe back up through the air and slamming it down this time, slicing through, so that his foot came away from the body; blood spilled out onto the frost, and she bent down to peel his sock off.

She wrapped his foot very tightly in the bin liner; pressing the foot and ankle into a corner of the bag and pulling the material flush around it. Then she made a knot very close to the back of the ankle, so that there could be no trapped air.

🍴

11. It might be useful to keep a little record. How did he die? Was it during a row? On a scale of 1 to 10, what sort of a row? What, or who, was also involved? What about the neighbors?
12. Are you on a street or out in the country?
13. Did anyone hear you?
14. Any neighbors who might be particularly susceptible to melodrama? Be mindful of determined, pursed lips and/or ashen faces, and beady eyes on a cold suburban street. Anyone out there unaware of

the depth of their own anger, or unable to experience it in any sort of appropriate way, will be dreaming of a situation like this. It could keep them alive for years.

15. The world is full of parasites.
16. Keep your curtains closed.
17. Did you also chuck china, glass, or try to kick down a wall? Was the dog involved? Lashing out at animals during an argument is common, particularly when losing an argument to a passive-aggressive other.
18. Is there an injury of your own that you must also attend to now that he is in the freezer?
19. Did you get kicked, whacked, slammed in a door or throttled? If so, be vigilant. You don't want to find yourself being examined in hospital for a broken finger while there is human flesh in your teeth, throat and stomach.

She left the body bleeding over the hole and took the foot to the house and into the garage. She put it in the freezer, in between the *petits pois* and the spinach. Then she went one step further in her organization and fetched a white label from the same drawer of miscellaneous items in the kitchen. She wrote on the label, RIGHT FOOT, then pressed it onto the bag and put the freezer lid down.

Straight back outside, and all his clothes came off

then, his blue corduroy trousers with the faded knees, his black T-shirt and thin jumper; even his soft old tartan boxer shorts were carefully folded in a pile. She dragged him with the other leg so that she could take more of the stump off over the hole. Then the axe came down above the wrinkled right knee, where the skin had gone soggy. She took the axe up into the air and brought it down again into the bottom of his femur. This time the bone resisted, grabbed the steel and held. Lizzie felt something in her stomach then, a heave, and a rush of sweat to the temples and to the upper lip. She felt the panic, and her fear of the panic; so then she straightened up a little, holding the axe like a golf club while she took a big steadying breath.

She closed her eyes and pulled the axe out of the slit in his thigh, laying it carefully on the grass. Going to the shed for the saw, she put her gloved wrist to her upper lip knowing she was smearing blood all over her face.

But her legs had been working and she had known how to get the saw from the shed and stride back across the lawn. That was the strange thing. She had known how to carry on.

Jacob had pointed out quite early on in the marriage that Lizzie had an inability to be present in the moment. He said she didn't notice things. Not with all of her senses. On the contrary, though, all that oxygen made her feel high and alone out in the woods—so much so that coming in to curl up with the dog often felt like the sensible thing to do. It was pitiful, he said, how she never wanted to go to London, or do anything. They never went anywhere. He'd shouted: "Why can't we just throw the dog in the car and go hiking?"

She placed the ridged blade of the saw in the wound she'd made with the axe. The bone was thick and heavy—he'd not been good at sports—and she heard it splinter as the saw moved backwards and forward in the wound. She had deliberately not thought of the fleshy bits or the cutting feeling or the muggy butcher's smell in her nostrils. She knew then—out on the lawn that morning she really understood—that things could be boxed up in the mind, and there wasn't any pain to be managed but her own.

¶¶

20. Notice that little lift inside when you put the hand in the oven, as when putting new-season lamb in on a cold night in March.

21. Parboil a handful of new potatoes to be crushed into the tray with the juice of a lemon and some mint leaves from the garden.

22. Resist the urge to put in a lot of garlic. Cook as normal.

23. Spare time can be spent thinking about where you are going to go when this month is over. Remember

that you might be able to do this in less than a month. It could take a week. You have given yourself a month so as not to feel distressed.

24. Give yourself breaks. Little treats. A can of Coke. The odd cigarette. Hot-water bottles. Bubble baths. A decent bottle of wine.

25. It is going to take you less than a month. Think a fortnight. Think three weeks max.

Back in the kitchen, Lizzie took the hand out of the oven and tipped it straight onto a plate. She breathed and looked, but she couldn't leave it like that, with the skin all black and blistered, and the fingernails still on. Even with the potatoes crushed, and gathered nicely around it. Which actually made everything worse; the potatoes so fresh and small, and the hand charred and risen up, with the fingers flattened at the ends and curling in a bit in a weak, shriveled claw. Even after she'd sprinkled the *mange-tout* like camouflage, it was still Jacob's right hand. She took the vegetables away, slid his hand off the plate, and put it back on the chopping board. Then she took the mallet and gave it a big smack, so that the back of the hand burst open revealing sinews of white meat and sharp, popping veins. Lizzie gagged and reached across for his spinning wedding ring, and then she leaned back, and closed her eyes.

♞♟

26. Heap broken bits onto a plate and make a stack with *mange-tout* and baby corn.

27. Dollop a great spoon of red-currant jelly, and add another sprinkle or two of best-quality sea salt.

28. Carry your plate to the table and sit on a chair. Put wine on the table, and a newspaper or magazine. Strategically place a colorful coffee-table book (that one you have of woodland birds?) so that you can keep your eye on the pictures.

29. Turn the radio on (you won't be at the stage yet where sounds are like a scraping sensation in your ear) or grab a felt-tip to scribble on the paper while you eat. All you need to be doing is arranging things in such a way as to make the eating of human flesh a little bit easier. As you eat, therefore, you might like to read the words aloud, or riotously pull pages out of the magazine and focus your hearing on the rip.

30. Alternatively, look down at your plate, at what you are doing, and try to understand. You will want to vomit. You can do that, and then eat. Chances are that if you look now you'll be better off later. You'll have begun the emotional processing. Better in the long run. Much better than if you look away in the scary bits.

31. Listen, though, looking away is a reflex. It's normal, and human, and absolutely fine. It's what we do all the time. You don't have to adopt the warrior pose while the pieces are in the oven, or sit like Shiva. Remember, a Buddhist wouldn't do this. Or anything like this. What you are doing is more challenging, more stressful than anything anyone has ever done before.

Lizzie used her knife and fork at first, with a spoon set out for sorbet after, but the cutlery was put down after a minute or two, and the dog given the odd tidbit under the table. She nibbled her husband's roasted fingers, as if from a rib, and she cracked the smaller bones of the thumb while frowning hard.

She watched the clock. It was almost nine. The heating had gone off, but the radiator was still warm. Under the table, Rita was sitting up and alert. From time to time she shifted on her paws, knocking her skull on the wood as if to remind Lizzie that she was still there.

🍴

32. Begin a stockpot. Peel and roughly chop one carrot, one onion. Chop one stalk of celery and soften carrots, onions and celery with black peppercorns,

dried bay leaf, fresh parsley stalks, a sprig of
fresh thyme.

33. Let the stockpot simmer on the stove for a few
days. Let the bones get nice and soft, then simply
lift them out with a ladle and purée in a blender before returning to the pot.

34. As you work through the freezer you can simply add
leftovers and season. You will build up something
really delicious and flavorsome that you could use
perhaps for a final meal.

3

Lizzie tipped the hand bones that were left on her plate into the stock—she was using the old casserole dish—and then she stacked the plates on the side. The stock was a bit smelly, so she opened the back door to let air into the kitchen, and she waited there, in the doorway, while the food inside her went down.

After the sorbet, she sat for a while at the table, looking at the tiny ceramic geese with their heads bent forward over the sill. They'd come in a set from her ship-broker boss before she'd got made redundant from the office in Guildford, and she'd painted the scarves with a tiny brush from some pots of ceramic paint. Twenty years on from art school, and she'd felt like a fool doing that, and Jacob had sniggered when he'd come in to see what she was doing.

Lizzie climbed up onto the sink in her slippers and shoved the little geese to the side with her foot. She reached up for the curtain pole and pulled the end off, stepping back into the basin and letting the curtains slide to the floor. The curtains had come from his parents' house. Like so much else here they were old and musty and unloved.

*　　*　　*

LP was short for loo paper. It was also Lizzie Prain. Not that it mattered. But had he meant to include her on his list? Had he been thinking of something to buy for her, some little trinket perhaps to show her he'd been thinking of her and wanted to reconnect? More likely it was loo paper. Or because he had something to say. "Tell LP I'm going to London this afternoon to see Joanna," for example. Not that he'd have bothered to say anything if that was the case. He never had. He just went and thought nothing of it. There was nothing left. There had barely been anything there at all. Beyond their mutual need for someone, something, to cling to.

You could see from the fridge how things had been: empty, pretty much, and the shelves smeary and old. They'd not been gregarious. Or had people round. The ceilings were low, and the house, on its dripping bend in the lane, was too small, they'd felt, for entertaining. And it wasn't signposted well. It wasn't his fault, of course. He'd been given the house by his aunt Jane, who'd left it to him in her will. Happily, he'd come down from the north of England, with a box full of punk records and some old curtains, to take it on.

Lizzie took the old jars from the fridge, rinsed them at the sink, gave each a good wash with her fingers, and then placed them in the recycling box by the back door. The rubber gloves came off with a snap. Being practical was paramount. First thing in the morning, she thought, she would go round the house adding things to the box.

　　　🍴

35.　Keep a pad of fresh white paper on the table. Or a ring-bound notebook. Make lists of things you will need in the fridge. You're trying not to spend money, but do bear in mind that you will crave quite bland things after a few days. Porridge oats? Rice? Look for these in the cupboard and put them on the sideboard to counter the feeling of meat. Millet is known for its calming, grounding properties. There's a health-food shop in Farnham. Why not pop in there and pick up a bag of millet? You could combine it with a visit to the bank to discuss the joint account.

36.　A bit of crisp celery might be nice.

37.　Lemons.

38.　Clementines.

39.　Keep the kitchen clean at all times. Evidence needs to be removed moment by moment. Put cigarette ends in the bin. Clean up after yourself. Put dishcloths in the dishwasher with the dirty dishes so that they can be thoroughly cleaned in very hot water. Wipe down the work surfaces.

40.　Put the dog's bed in your bedroom if it helps you to feel less alone.

41. You are, by the way, at this moment in your life, completely alone. Like wandering in the Antarctic of human experience.
42. Worth remembering next time you feel the pang.
43. This is only loneliness.
44. And it will pass.

She wouldn't actually say that she'd done him a favor. His depression had brought him closer to death on several occasions than she'd ever been in her own life, but it wasn't clear if he'd ever really meant to do himself in.

There was the time she'd found him trying to hang himself from a tree by standing on paint cans he'd put on the wall at the bottom of the garden. Possibly he'd been doing it for attention. He'd looked back at the house to see her standing in the kitchen window. Then, after a while, he'd given up. He'd let his neck out of the noose and come back in, smiling, to put the kettle on.

He'd not been able to understand his own moods. He'd pushed the downs into weird crazed little ups with a vicious smile and eyes bright and hard as buttons. An instantaneous walling-off. And one of the things Lizzie felt she might get on eating him was insight into his character. When the freezer was emptied she thought she might be able to write down at least one thing Jacob had learned about life through living with her. Patience wasn't one of them. Not the sort that was revealed in conversation when people stopped thinking and speaking about themselves and simply sat there listening. Or nodding, as Lizzie had often done while Jacob talked. Patience, like generosity, came as much from an ability to feel love for a person as it did from a need to be loved in return, and she wasn't sure that, once they'd moved in together and settled—she in a house that gave her shelter from the bewildering world, he to a routine of meals made on time and a person to help him out—they had really needed to *feel* each other's love. In the beginning, of course, it hadn't been like that. They'd needed to feel the love to know they were doing the right thing in being together. They'd both been fierce: he in his misanthropy, she in her pragmatism. But then, like most people, they'd taken whatever it was that had brought them together for granted. Or stopped, for all the inexplicable reasons others did, being able to show it. Lizzie hadn't been particularly patient or generous with him either. She'd rarely commented on his pieces. When he'd not liked something she'd cooked, she'd put it in the fridge and served it up the next night—exactly the same format—just to make it known that fussy eating wasn't an option in her kitchen. If he didn't appreciate her efforts to experiment then he might as well go hungry. She hadn't been patient, either, with the trips to London in the car.

They didn't have children, and even though they'd agreed on their wedding night, face to face, under the covers, that they now had a duty of care to one another, he had later reneged on that, and said that leaving at any point, if one felt trapped, was absolutely essential, and that they should both just feel able to go. Up until the redundancies and the thing with the noose and the paint cans and the fetching in of the punk records from the shed, Lizzie had felt that she loved Jacob, if not intensely, then quite fairly. He'd given her shelter and opened up his home, and if things had gone a bit weird from time to time in the first two decades, the rest of the time they'd been all right—not talkative, but not despairing either. She'd watched a lot of television; and he'd fiddled about in his shed. There had been the occasional disappearance: his "walkabout" wandering off into the night with a rucksack of supplies. It wasn't exactly testing terrain, but toughing it out in the cold beyond the wall at the bottom of the garden had nonetheless stirred something in him. The first time he'd gone off into the woods for two nights, he'd come back excited to see her, and had come up behind her and wrapped his arms around her waist. That was rare. She'd stepped back on his toes, and then hung her apron up and gone alone to the Dog and Duck in the village, sitting up at the bar, where she'd ordered a bottle of wine and read a magazine with her raincoat tied around her waist. She'd not been able to express herself. It wasn't just him. And she had wanted to have sex that night. Out of relief that he had come back and the twinge of pleasure she'd got when he wrapped his arms around her waist. They must have been young, in their thirties then, and she'd gone instead to the pub in a huff and listened to Teri behind the bar talk some rubbish about Spain.

Lizzie knew that Jacob had loved her ability to bring him down to earth. She'd had, for him, a comforting grasp of a much more commonplace reality—brought up not in a big house in the north as he was, but by a single mother in a boarding house above a shop on the drizzly south coast. Jacob knew he could roam from the cottage because Lizzie was practical—poverty had made her that way, he'd said—and there would always be food on the table, and a bed upstairs with sheets that were clean. Their home, as she'd pointed out one evening by knocking on a wall, wasn't caving in, and she, his loving wife, was sitting very still at the table with her eyes open and looking straight at him while holding up an oatcake with a slice of Brie, which managed to convey, she felt, that she wasn't going anywhere, things weren't running to cheese as he saw them in his mind. They were going to be all right. She did love him. Almost from the word go. Quite soon after he'd taken her in. He knew that. Her loyalty had been as fierce as the Ridgeback's.

$$\text{\textbardbl}$$

45. Codependents suffer from low self-esteem and
make excuses for other people. They are usually

women and tend to become the wives of alcoholics, workaholics, manic-depressives, plain depressives and passive-aggressives.

46. Codependents exhaust themselves trying to please.

47. Either one is a fan of labels or one isn't. They can be useful during the early stages when one is trying to cut loose and press on. Later on, when the healing begins, it will be necessary to detach from the label in order to find out where you actually are. You may have to go through many permutations.

48. Making excuses for his behavior, or lack of, during consumption of his corpse will not do you any favors. None at all.

49. As much as possible, switch off the thinking brain and go through the motions. Eat, shit, sleep. Repeat this mantra to yourself when you wake in the morning and when you go to sleep at night.

50. Eat. Shit. Sleep.

It was late when Lizzie finished her tidying in the kitchen and fished the right foot out of the freezer to thaw. She put some clean water out for Rita and switched the kitchen lights off. Upstairs in the bathroom she washed her face and put her night cream on, and she wasn't bothered about what anyone else would think, she thought, as she rubbed her fingers in a circular motion on her cheeks and forehead. She'd made a decision: she wasn't going to prison for killing Jacob Prain. She was living again, on borrowed time, and there was something thrilling about that. A sort of "fuck them all" feeling. It was as if, in the act of killing him, and getting on with what came next, she'd smashed up the old concerns, and now life was coming richly in. She was feeling completely calm. Even when she thought of his body on the lawn and the axe going through the air with that whistling sound, she was able to feel contained. She lay back in bed and rubbed her fingers together and felt the energy fizzing in her fingertips. She was quite still. There was no pain in any part of her. It's shock, she told herself, and then she switched the bedside lamp off and wriggled down beneath the duvet.

Tom

She had red lipstick on. That was what was different about her. She came and found me—I was unloading compost out the front—and she asked about tongs for the barbecue and rubber gloves. I said I could help her with both, and we went inside.

"My husband left me," she said, just like that, in front of the drills.

I stopped and turned around. I didn't say anything. I looked at her. Then I looked back at the drills. I wanted to burp, to release what felt like a blockage, or heartburn, in my chest. I felt a tugging sensation, like there was a thing inside her that would get out if it could and pull on my sleeve. I wanted to say, *I think I'd leave you too. I think I'd have to.* That was the thought that came to me. I didn't, though. Of course not. I just stood beside her. Her hands were gripping her cloth bag. I put my hands in my pockets. We looked at the drills. Then I felt the tears. I took a tissue out of my pocket as the tears spilled down my face.

She asked if I wanted to go to the café to get a cup

of coffee with her. I nodded and said that I'd go and ask my boss if I could take a break. It was early, around ten. I tried to walk away looking relaxed, with an arm swinging at the side.

I met her back in the café. She was sitting in the window, very upright with that frizz of hair. There were two cups of coffee on the table, and a plate with a slice of carrot cake. She was staring forward, as if there were someone sitting opposite her. She pushed the plate of cake towards me. I sat down and curled over my elbows on the table and said something about being someone who believed in releasing emotion and how that often got in the way of my work. I said something about being a sensual person. I laughed a bit. Lizzie seemed startled by what had happened back at the drills. She didn't say a word.

"I cry a lot," I said. "And there isn't always a reason. It's fine."

She turned to look out at the "Pick Your Own" field. There was someone out there, bending down in the rows.

"Won't be any strawbs," I said, trying to be cheerful, to make conversation. It was a thick, overcast sky.

"How long were you and your husband together?" I asked.

"Thirty years," she said.

I nodded. That didn't mean anything to me. How could it? I was barely an adult. Thirty was a number. I didn't know anything about being with anyone for any length of time and, anyway, I thought most people probably overdid it and let things go stale.

"How did you meet him?"

"He put an advert up at the art school. He'd broken his leg. He needed someone to help him. Thought it might be a way to meet someone."

"You mean it wasn't true?"

"No," she said. "It was true. He had broken his leg, and it was a slow recovery thing, and he did need some help. As you know, there isn't a shop or anything that you can get to easily from ours with a broken leg. But he did think it would be a way to meet someone."

"Nice," I said, and grinned. "Kill two birds."

Lizzie tried to smile. It was more a wince.

"It's March," she said, suddenly, which was when I noticed the redness—a rash—at the corners of her mouth. I understood that the last weeks had been difficult for her, and I felt bad for making the scene with the tears.

"It is possible that I'm feeling this for you," I said, and I looked up through the top of my eyes. Lizzie looked back at me. After a while, she said: "You barely know me."

"No."

I went back to staring at the redness at the corners of her mouth.

We drank our coffee. She closed her eyes when she drank. She didn't touch the cake.

We sat there feeling awkward. Then she said she'd get the things she came for.

4

🍴

51. Lean meat is mostly water, so try to switch the fan on your oven off, if possible, to avoid evaporation. Even the best joints can become tough and dry if cooked beneath a whirring fan.

52. Take the meat out of the fridge and let it stand on a sideboard, to get to room temperature before you start. Don't be afraid to open the oven, once it's in, to see how it's doing. Press the meat with a finger to see if it is soft, springy or hard. With chicken, a knife should be slid in between the thigh and body to see if the juices run clear. With a man's foot, you might like to do the same just above the ankle bone, or between his big toe and the next one along.

53. Let the meat rest under foil for at least ten minutes before carving.

*   *   *

"Nothing lasts," Lizzie whispered, standing in the garden on Friday night with a small brandy, and a pile of burning curtains in a bonfire on the lawn.

His foot had been lying salted and sideways in a roasting tray for two and a half hours, but on a lower heat than the hand had been, so the skin was more coffee-colored than black, and the meat was softer. She'd taken the pink gloves off and wedged them between her knees while she scraped tiny slivers of flesh off the ankle bone and the bridge, and from the heel, and added them to a hot ginger stir-fry with rice noodles, the rest of the *mange-tout*, sweet chili sauce and half a red cabbage.

It had started to rain now and Lizzie was pleased. The rain would fill up the hole and give the grass a really good dousing. The *Farnham Herald* was still there for reading, and she was feeling well. In general, she had been fine all week. Her wits had been about her. Right from the moment she'd gone down on the grass to check his pulse. Ten minutes earlier she'd been standing in the bedroom window upstairs, still in her dressing gown, watching him dig. Oak, he'd wanted. For its longevity and rotund glory. She'd got dressed. Ten seconds to drop the dressing gown on the floor, reach for her jeans from the cupboard. Over the nightie. Less than a minute. Through to the kitchen, out the back door and into the garden. Bringing the spade down on the top of his head. Then the small mental adjustment. Doing it again. Nothing from him. He was fifty-five. She'd expected a reaction; she'd wanted a fight. Nothing had come. He was down. She'd sniffed and touched his hair.

Like the girl she was before she'd got caught up with him, and her brain had started to cleave to his, Lizzie had stood up then and looked about her. Like the girl who might have done other things, the girl who'd walked instead into the garden on the first day and felt that she could probably manage to be here while she figured out what else there was, she'd taken in the details. The garden was hidden from the lane by the house, and completely surrounded by tall dark trees. She was the same person, it was the same garden, and the two views bookended everything in between. With the body on the lawn she'd looked quickly at the garden chairs. Then up at the trees.

Now she was sitting at the kitchen table with a plate of his left foot, the skin of which was thick and tough, the skin on the sole so thick she hadn't been able to score it, and had left it sitting in the pan like an inner sole from an old shoe. There was a slick of yellow-white fat under the heel and under the toe. While she ate the stir-fry she glanced at the paper and studied the schoolchildren lined up in a photograph on the front.

She went back to the roasting tin on the sideboard, and peered at the crunchy bones like a bracelet in the arch. She scraped a little meat from his toes with her knife and fork and held the pieces in her mouth; there was a porky taste, which was all right. So she scraped another bit of toe and held it out in her fingers for the dog, who devoured it gratefully and licked her lips and wagged her tail for more. Rita liked the little bits of meat that could be flaked away from the bones, but she wasn't going for the sole either. She simply sniffed it on the plate put down, and let her tongue go out towards it, then withdrew, sucking ruefully back into her lips.

"Like rubber?" whispered Lizzie, and she bent down to remove the plate, giving Rita a handful of dry biscuits from the bag she'd taken out of the bin in the garage and brought into the kitchen.

She and Rita did what they could with the foot, and then Lizzie hammered up the bones on the chopping board and put the shards and the fat that was left over in the stockpot with bouquet garni and celery. She added two pints of water. She would need the clothes peg on again while it boiled and simmered and this she would have to do with candles burning before she went to bed; then reduce with wine, blend again in the mixer and reduce for an hour more till she got a fine golden stock which could be stored in a Tupperware.

*　*　*

In the garage on Saturday morning, Lizzie put her finger to the light switch and waited in darkness while the overhead light came on.

Several months ago she had tried to clear the garage and the shed. She got some of the old sculptures out to take to the dump. There was a foot he'd made of plaster. It was sitting on the old TV, close to the door. She'd carried it to the bottom of the garden. He was sitting in a deckchair, watching her.

"Ah," he said. "I've thought about doing that."

She walked past him with the cast in the air.

"I'm going to convert the shed into an office."

He could have done it. It was big enough; it was a double-sized shed, like an Alpine cabin, with a step up.

"Cakes," he said, watching her bend over the oven to take one out about a month after the shop closed down. Jacob's Antiques, in Guildford, hadn't been *his* antiques but Tim Smith's, and Tim had given it Jacob's name because he felt it was a good one, stronger, warmer. Jacob worked there five days a week. "A good job for a budding sculptor," he used to say, sort of joking, though it wasn't the most unlikely. He worked there for many years. Then the shop closed down and Tim went to France.

"Cakes?" she'd said, putting the fruit sponge on the table in the bread tin.

He'd been making suggestions about what he could

do, since he didn't like going to the job center to collect his benefits. Three years ago now to the very week, and she'd cut him a slice of fruit cake then and said she'd think about it. She'd not been working either and things at home were disastrous with both of them being around. Both in their late forties. Inertia had come into the house as if it were being belched and yawned from a mouth under the floorboards.

"What with our brilliant oven!" he said, showing his yellow teeth.

"It is a great oven," she said, and he put his arms around her then. She felt the hope rise in her like sap. You needed something, one thing of your own to do, however small; and Lizzie had known that she could cook, and bake, and that she could do these things with love.

PRAIN CAKES

or

WOODLAND CAKES

At the Dog and Duck, they said: Great! The message spread. It could be lucrative. And Jacob and Lizzie went to the pub a few times and tried to fit in. Up at the bar, some of the local folk were talking as if they'd all known each other for years.

"The Prains are going to make cakes, love."

"Got a van?"

"We'll use the car," Lizzie said, climbing onto the bar stool in a pair of tight brown trousers.

"Be good to be working again," she whispered to her husband, who was standing beside her, nodding into his beer. For a moment there it had felt warm and loving around him, and spacious.

"Long time off now."

"No one wants to be out of work, do they?"

"Not now."

"No one wants to be scratching around."

"Thing is, no one says you're going to get depressed, do they?"

"That's right."

"No one says what's coming."

"How can they know?"

"That's right."

They even heard about it up at the farm. She took some fairy cakes with her one evening in a tin. To confirm it was happening, and ask them to spread the word around. It wasn't a great meeting. Not ideal for someone starting out on a venture. Lizzie was met at the door and not welcomed in. Later, she imagined the cakes flying through the air on the back of Erik's fist. "He's just the sort of man to do things like that," she said to Jacob, who disagreed and said, "That's a bit unfair."

But Lizzie had known from before, from the way Erik shouted at the dog and the cows when she'd done the babysitting, that things were hard up at the farm. As with last time, she came away feeling tight in the chest and hurried past the same shiny saloon car parked black and silent in the drive. With the front seats pushed right back. Erik at the door and Barbara behind him with her huge face and a small purple nose. Half of her coming forward and the other half held back in the corridor, a wry, secretive, disastrous smile keeping them all, one felt, from a harm she couldn't articulate.

But Tom said Lizzie's cakes were really good. He'd appeared in the doorway, squeezed past his parents, tall and pretty, and put an arm out to get one from the tin.

"Wow!" he said, chewing and licking and smiling at her. "Wowwow!"

So people knew she could do it.

Someone at the pub said: "Always knew there was something creative about you."

"Who? Me?"

"Yeah, you. Always knew you were a bright spark."

People drank to her health.

"There's that lovely picture of yours they sell in the craft center in Seale. The goose one."

"The partridge."

"Yeah, the partridge."

Jacob said: "A real beauty, that one." It had been a beauty. When she'd first come to the house she'd wandered up and down the lane taking photographs. She had loved the way, when she went out at night with the head torch on, the elephant grass had stood out so white and shocking, like images from a real swamp in

Florida or somewhere. She'd tried hard to capture the light peeking through the leaves in the lane, the briefness of it, how it would wink and chase the car. In the early days, when his leg was better and he'd taken up driving again, she'd sat in the front with her head back on the headrest and gazed up at the trees. There had been a sense of the numinous then. She'd felt the love inside her, and all around her in the lane, and she'd taken some pictures to capture that.

Some people had said it might be hard. Just the two of them out in the woods like that, going into business together. They might not make it in this market.

But how hard could it be? Wedding cakes, birthday cakes, anniversaries, funerals.

Easy-peasy.

She made them. Sleeves rolled up in the kitchen, flowers in a jug on the sill. Jacob took orders on the telephone. He washed up, and then he delivered the cakes in the Volvo. He got lost, a second time. A fortieth birthday in Weybridge. Just up the A3. A pub not far from the exit. He didn't know why.

"Don't know," he said when she asked the next morning. She was trying to find the right time to inquire.

"How could you have got lost, Jacob? The directions were so clear."

"Shitty map, though."

Lizzie went back to weeding the garden. Then the customer rang and said how much they'd be charging for the inconvenience of all those phone calls from the party and someone having to buy chocolate cake from the supermarket right in the middle of the speech.

Meanwhile, for supper in the kitchen it was shepherd's pie, and the salmon thing in a pastry roll, the leek and potato soup he'd always given a thumbs-up. Cottage pie. A good roast. Pork, chicken, beef. They'd never had much lamb, except on a special occasion. More as a treat. But British in the main: food enjoyed in childhood was food enjoyed always. He'd liked things the same. He'd worn his boots till the soles flapped off, then they'd got replaced at Clarks in Guildford; and every Easter, for five years, he'd hired a van, and driven a sculpture of his own creation up to a woman called Joanna for her pleasure garden in London.

"Three hundred and fifty quid," he said, coming back from the first time, striding in. His jeans had holes in the knees.

At the antiques shop in Guildford he told his striking customer that sculpture was really his thing. It was what he would have done, he said.

They smoked outside on the street, Lizzie imagined, and laughed.

Joanna said, "Will you bring me something?"

That was what he reported.

Lizzie asked: "What did she wear?"

"What do you mean, what did she wear?"

"What kind of thing?"

"What do you mean, what kind of thing?" he said, milking it, pouting a little, inwardly proud. "Black," he said. "Leather jacket. Little leather skirt."

Lizzie said, "Leather skirt?"

"She says I should follow my heart."

Ah well, Joanna would have to do without his little creations now. There was no way of contacting him. She'd probably try, once or twice, and then tire of it soon enough. Joanna was a busy woman in London, and busy women let people slip away to sea, Lizzie had found. Jacob Prain wasn't a priority. Him in his little woodland house, out in the dark somewhere, ruminating on the life he might have made.

They'd both been ruminators, though. That was part of the problem. She went back to that Monday morning and saw herself in her jeans, with her legs flying back under her nightie, and her hands on the wheelbarrow she was pushing across the lawn. She saw herself reaching under his shoulders and swiveling the body around on the grass, falling back on her arse and then over him once with the strain. She was able to tilt the body by lifting his shoulders and wedging her knee against the top of his back, allowing the blood to flow from his leg stumps into the hole. She had tried to bring his leg stumps together but they splayed back open, leaving his shriveled privates exposed. The hole soon filled to the brim with blood and she let the body back down on the grass and then used the hose to wash the blood from his stumps and from her fingers.

She had used the axe then, to take his hands off at the wrists and wrap these, and then the arms, which left her with just the torso to deal with. And the head, of course. Each of his organs, she decided, would need to be individually wrapped and labeled so that she could quickly distinguish in the aftermath what was what.

She knew it was going to take a little more sherry to still the shaking hands, so she went back in for the bottle to keep beside her, and she had a swig before bending down to bag and tie everything up. Every bag was pulled tight and neatly tied. Then she pushed them all over to the freezer in the wheelbarrow.

She let the dog out. Rita sniffed and wagged and licked, then disappeared, leaping the fence behind the shed and going in search of her own, smaller kill.

Lizzie felt her hair coming away from its clip and she knew she looked mad, with the pale frizz and the blood all over her face. Her adrenaline was really pumping, and in its wake was a new strength, as if a human being had always known, deep down, how to get on with the business of doing away with another.

Determination. That was what Jacob said was lacking in her when she came back from the interview at the shipbroker's.

"I can't help thinking you should have stuck it out at

art school," he said, and Lizzie wondered if he felt responsible for her change of direction.

"I'm not going to make it as an artist, though. It's perfectly obvious, Jacob. I don't have the talent."

"It's not that," he said. "You're not as bad as you think. But you lack determination. It's as if you missed that piece," he said, with a smile. "Ego, and determination, to do things for yourself."

Which was better than being a hard-arsed bollockbreaker, she replied. To which he suggested she relax.

And thinking about that out on the grass while chopping him up that Monday made Lizzie pause, and take the gloves off, and spritz them with the hose. Then she sat back on her ankles with her hands splayed out flat on her knees.

She had to check herself then, to know that she was all right.

She gave up the gloves. They were in a terrible state and made her hands sweat. She went on with her bare skin and turned what was left of him over onto its front and positioned it so that the head with its white neck was facedown on the inside of a bin liner she'd pressed into the bloody hole. She knelt down beside the neck and splayed her fingers where she wanted to make an incision with the saw. The axe might have been quicker, but she feared its abrupt violence now, and felt that the head required specific care.

She placed the ridged blade against the skin, feeling

in her own neck a stab of pain as the blade went in. Into her mind came the blue-gray eyes she had known—they were staring into the hole now—so dark on some days they'd gone a scary slaty black, and she got a sudden mysterious whiff of his aftershave and tobacco.

The only sound in the frosty garden was from the saw as her hand moved it back and forth minutely in his neck and eased through the top of his spine. The marrow was something to bear in mind, and she'd not expected to see it quite like that, with all the white threads coming out as the head tumbled into the bag. She tied a knot and went to the freezer and placed the bag inside, with a label, HEAD, pressed on and smoothed.

She had tried to do every major chop over the hole he'd been digging, and in most cases she'd succeeded. Blood had gone right into the soil and turned it the color of aubergines.

🍴

54. You were absolutely right to keep spritzing the body with water from the hose.
55. But try not to think back. I believe it's a strategy— this glancing back all the time—that the mind has adopted to keep you from the task at hand.
56. Gently come back to what you are doing. Don't worry about the time, or any sounds you might hear

in the lane. You are quite secluded in these woods, and the trees and darkness will give you the protection you need at the moment.

She'd used the saw to get through his waist, lining up with his belly button. She went in through the downy hair and punctured his stomach. The juices sprang into the air and squirted her face and made her vomit. She had not known a smell like that—she was really shaking then—and knew she was on the verge of passing out, so she stuck her jaw forward as she wheeled him over the grass and into the garage for the final labeling and freeze.

Lizzie had watched a lot of television in her life— probably more than most women of her age, he'd told her—even so, *real* life, the one she'd suddenly jumped into the picture for, wasn't so spectacular. The body was softer and less bloody than on the TV, and leaping up behind the axe to get through his femur, for example, wasn't necessary. There were clots flung out on the ground that she scraped with a trowel, but everything was hosed down by four in the afternoon, and the hose was coiled back on the wall, the freezer shut.

Saturday morning. Lizzie opened the lid of the freezer and took two chunky bags out.

"What the hell," she whispered to herself. She'd had

such a good start. A fortnight was surely more than enough to do this in.

She put the pink gloves in the bin. They made her hands hot and itchy and she would need to get some better ones. From the cupboard beside the fridge she took down the ring binder and found the number of the telephone company. A man had come and installed the router so that they had been able to make better use of the Internet. He'd improved their speed, just before she lost her job.

It was still her voice. Of course it was. It was just a regular Saturday morning and she was speaking on the telephone.

Lizzie dialed the number and waited. They could cut the phone line whenever she was ready. The man was cheery. He said that was absolutely fine.

🍴

57. So far you have eaten your husband's right hand and his left foot.

58. Give yourself some credit for achievement.

59. Keep up the notes. Remember when he said that your cakes were probably fundamentally poor owing to a lack of imagination in their creator? To which you'd replied, of course, that it doesn't take imagination to follow a recipe.

60. Might be worth having a little look at the knives. Are they nice and sharp?

61. Handy to have a good, sharp fruit knife for skinning fiddly bits like fingers and toes. A bread knife will get you through anything but with a bit of mess. Goes without saying of course that the carving knife needs to be in pristine condition. Once sharpened, try storing your knives in a cloth pouch in a separate part of the cutlery drawer. Others have used cork. The principle is the same.

62. As night falls on the third or fourth day, you may feel a little bit weary and a little bit afraid. I'd light a good fire in the living room and sit yourself down in there with a cup of tea or glass of white wine. Keep the curtains drawn against the dark and random little peepers. Let your spirits sink for a moment or two if you sense they are going that way. No need to fight the moods. Let them be as they are, and rest in the knowledge that you'll pop back up.

"Nothing lasts," Jacob had said about the cold she'd got from standing outside the house waiting for him on a damp, freezing Sunday afternoon. He had said to get to the house at two o'clock. The bus had dropped her off in Puttenham and then she'd walked, out past the pub with the hanging baskets and the field with the horse.

She'd waited on the porch all afternoon. In the rain, he

struggled out of the taxi, and held out the door key. He limped forward with a crutch. She got up from her huddle and went towards him, stretching out an arm. She introduced herself.

"I'm really sorry," he said, gently. Then he put his head down, and winced.

Which was the moment, she now thought, if there had to be a precise one, that she'd got sucked in. That warmth in "sorry," the head down, the wince. Softness and sorrow and pity. She'd wanted to help him. In helping, she was able to go somewhere, to slide right into the warmth she would make.

"Thanks," he said. They walked together up to the door. "I'm really sorry for keeping you."

They sat in the kitchen.

She watched him moving around. He lit a fire in the living room, and made a pot of tea that they drank with his tin of digestive biscuits between them. He was charming.

He didn't say why he'd been held up. It didn't seem to matter by then. She felt the cold coming on. Something inside her had surrendered already. She had given up wanting to be at art school, where everyone seemed set on making a point. Here she could take some photographs and look after him. She could be away from the world.

He was young, yet talking softly, and stooping, as if he were sixty.

"I wanted to be a sculptor," he'd said. "It's what I would have done."

He hadn't said: "It's what I would have done if things had been different." He hadn't tried to lay the blame on anyone else. And she had turned her face to that and smiled. No resentment clogging up the air here then. A little bit of kindness. Rolled-up soft trousers, even in winter. And fresh air. It hadn't occurred to her that he might know how angry he was, or who he was angry with.

Nothing lasts, she said to herself, standing out in the garden now in a woolen hat and coat and scarf. She switched the torch on and aimed it at the trees.

The thigh was vast. She had it in a bin liner on the garden table, and she stood for a long time looking at it as if she were planning to take a photograph. She drank a glass of white wine, and she looked at the thigh from every angle; she stood back and admired it, as he had done, occasionally, with hers.

Like the first time they'd gone to bed.

"Can you just sit on the bed, like that, on your knees, so that I can look at the shape?"

She'd done as he asked.

In the beginning, she always did what he asked her to do. He had a house; and she didn't. Partly, though, she'd done it because it turned her on. Being his object was a way out of feeling—at the moment when she might have begun to feel the intimacy, he did something like this, he made her an object, which gave her an excuse to distance herself. What a relief, to sit on his bed, to kneel like that without any clothes on. What a relief to run her hands down her front with her head down. She wouldn't have to hug him then, not while he was over there slumped in the armchair. She wouldn't have to wrap her arms around him and tell him how she really felt, which was close to love, certainly.

She walked around the garden table sizing up his thigh. She felt a sudden searing pain in her own thigh and kept putting a hand to it, rubbing around the hip. The front of her apron was dusted with flour from the potato croquettes she'd been making first thing.

It was almost seven o'clock. If she was firm enough with herself—if she applied all she had to herself as she might have done to a child—there was a chance she would be all right. The trick was to breathe slowly, and go with each moment as it presented itself.

She would hack through the femur with an axe and cook it in slices on the barbecue. Some of it she would be able to nestle down in the charcoal and it could cook away until she was ready to add the bones to another stockpot. She threw back the last few drops of wine.

She selected some spice jars from the kitchen and brought them out into the garden on a tray. She lit a cigarette and set the tray down beside the five slices of thigh and bent down on her knees using a fresh bin liner to keep herself dry. In the torchlight she opened up the spice jars, using first a teaspoon, then her fingers, to sprinkle cumin and coriander, nutmeg and cinnamon, fennel, basil, ginger. She really went for it this time, opening up the jars and letting the contents just fall on. Saffron, celery salt. What did it matter? She was leaving here—she'd be gone soon: she could tip the whole lot on his thigh and on the grass and let it all mix in.

It was as if she had stepped out of her own trajectory, and everything that had happened up to this point now seemed not irrelevant, but far less important; and all the old resentments had finally lost their cling. That they hadn't had a baby and had never got to the bottom of whose problem it was or why, that they'd stopped even talking about it after a while so that it just began to hang around her when she was out on her own in town looking at other people's kids, was no longer an issue. Children wouldn't be looked at. She'd left that need behind and stepped into a new realm. The territory was marked for her by avoidance and denial now. Survival and absolute simplicity was all there was left for her and suddenly she was at ease. She understood the boundaries. It was this, or nothing.

The barbecue was flaming; it was quite a party, she thought, standing back from the sparks.

Vitamins and nourishment; the goodness in Jacob, if there had been any at the end, was giving her the strength to get through this.

Life could be appreciated in individual moments. One could simply cut—with a sharp mental axe—impressions, thoughts, feelings, and trim off the bad bits, discard the fat.

She left the barbecue and walked towards the herbaceous border. She shone the torch right at it. The leaves on the rhododendron were a perfect deep green. She looked down at her neat white trainers and saw that there were little flecks of blood. But the trainers could be bleached, and washed; or they could be burned. If she decided the blood was a problem, if taking the trainers with her to Scotland with splashes of blood on the toes made her feel nervous, then the thing to do was simply to put them onto a bonfire of sticks on the lawn and burn them. While she was at it, she could burn the bedding and the actual bed. She could chop it up with the axe and use it for firewood. She could burn the trainers, burn the clothes and towels, and go to Scotland in her Wellington boots. That was it. She looked at her watch. Things were clear.

She used an oven glove and the tongs from the kitchen to lift a piece of thigh. She would need better gloves and proper tongs and she added these to her mental list while placing the slice down on a plate to cool. She glanced at her watch. Then she wrapped the slice in kitchen roll.

After the first bite, it was absolutely delicious. Like a hot piece of really flavorsome chicken, slightly charcoaled on the outside. She went into the kitchen for the ketchup and another bit of kitchen roll—he'd not been a good husband—and then she stepped back out to the garden. She would eat all the way through like this, she thought: all the pieces, wandering, moonlit and a little drunk, around the garden.

Tom

Lizzie agreed to give me a lift home. I realized as we got there that I didn't have my key. I knew that my grandfather would be at the farmhouse, but I didn't want to be there. I was happy talking to Lizzie on the way home in the car. I just wanted to stay like that. The heaviness had gone. In her car, she was more herself, and it felt like she was in control. I had no plans. But I didn't want to go to the farm. I pleaded with her. She was adamant that I couldn't come in. She said she was busy, that I couldn't even sit in the garden.

Then I told her what my grandfather had said about her husband disappearing, and her face began to change. Something passed across her brow and she became quite brisk and efficient. She said that I could come in. She said she was busy in the kitchen but that I could come in and see for myself that her husband had left her and that she was in the process of clearing out the house.

The house was really, weirdly empty. Much more than I thought it would have been. Even if the guy had done a runner I wouldn't have expected someone married for thirty years to clear their stuff out quite so fast. There was a patch of ash on the lawn out the back and I thought she'd probably been burning his things.

I thought she was brave. She showed me this receipt from an escort place in Guildford. She urged me to keep it, to show it to my grandfather so that he might stop his crazy imaginings. I told her that I wasn't going to take it and that she shouldn't feel she had anything to prove. "He's a mad old man," I told her. And she seemed happier after that.

I had a rest at her place and she went to make a cake. When I woke up she asked me if I would consider looking after the dog while she went to Scotland. She was glad that I'd come in after all because it had given her the idea. When it was done, she said, when it was fully cleaned up, I could stay there, and I could use the place as my own for a while. She said to bring my own bedding and towels. As we talked, she made these deliberate shrugging movements, as if it was all quite a casual arrangement, and I felt like she was someone who wasn't used to living like that at all, that by nature she was a much more cautious person who'd decided, since her husband had gone, to throw it all in the air and see what came back.

5

🍴

63. Don't start making comparisons with madwomen in history. You are not one of them.

64. Letting the brain get hold of a thought and run with it so that you are left sweating, panting, and groping for any available conclusion about the sort of a nutter you are is not going to be helpful.

65. Don't think, why did I do it? Think, what am I going to do about it now?

66. Pack an overnight bag. Put inside it: five pairs of pants, one for every day of the week. Two bras. A T-shirt. A long-sleeved thermal vest. Jumper. Jeans. Face cream. Flannel. Wash bag with shampoo, conditioner, toothpaste, toothbrush, mouthwash, dental floss, hand cream, eczema cream (best to use these things as and when you need to from now on and put them back in here). Keep this packed beside the bedroom door. Outside on the landing. It will reassure you that you are

on your way. It is also there if you feel you have to leave at any moment.

67. As for getting dressed, yesterday's outfit of jumper and jeans will do absolutely fine if that's what you feel like wearing. Who can tell you what you should be wearing to do this work? Some may choose a boilersuit, others a dress. What you were wearing yesterday is soft, uncomplicated, and on the floor. Slip back in.

68. Take the dog out for a walk.

69. Look at the grass underneath your boots. Think about how green it is. Look at the sludgy, wet, muddy mud all around the gate at the bottom of the garden. Look at the shine of rainwater on a leaf. Think about the ground under your feet. Can you feel the pine needles, hear them hiss and crunch together as you walk? What does it smell like? What does the air feel like on your cheek?

Lizzie stood in the dark lane and waited. It was Sunday morning. The feeling of heaviness in her chest had been there when she woke, and it was still there, a pushing sensation, insisting on something. She wanted to walk on up the lane towards the farm, but her legs felt stiff and heavy in her boots and she didn't know, all of a sudden, whether she would be seen. There was light coming through the trees. There would be air and light up on the common.

In a Saturday night feeding frenzy she had eaten her husband's whole thigh. She had not known a person could press so much meat in. Then she had gone to the fridge for more wine to wash down lump after lump of meat. She had been sick. Even so, she could feel the food as if it were in her throat; and even her head and cheeks were bloated.

The agent would say when she showed the house to people: "There's a lovely walk. You just go to the bottom of the garden, through the gate and you're out into the woods..."

Lizzie pulled her scarf around her neck, and turned through the woods. She went up the hill path, up towards the heath, her boots either side of the sandy ravine, and the dog disappeared into the bushes.

Up on the heath, Lizzie pulled a branch from the tree at the viewpoint, climbed down from the bench, and used the branch to whack the mud, lifting it up over her head and bringing it down with all her strength. The wind was blowing over the woods in the valley beneath, bringing the sound of the cars on the A31.

She heard a voice.

"Your dog's missing!"

It wasn't a question, but a madman out on surveillance. The voice was raspy. She knew who it was; and her heart thumped.

Lizzie looked back over the bracken to the little hand quivering near a white mouth. Her eyes dried quickly in the cold wind. He tried to shout to her again, but only a noise came out.

"Hello," she called, but the sound didn't seem to reach him. He didn't move. A wave of white hair was blowing across his head.

"I think at my place he's the only one sane," Tom Vickory had said. Lizzie looked at old Emmett. They were neighbors across hectares of woodland. In thirty years they'd had one lunch together.

"Your dog gone?" he shouted, and bounced on his heels.

"No," Lizzie called. "I brought her for a walk. She's over there!"

She forced a smile up into her cheeks. Old Emmett lifted his stick towards the oak tree with giant octopus arms that had been up here since the time of Henry VIII. "Over there!" she repeated. She made a waving gesture with a flat palm, and tramped away from the bench.

It wasn't clear how Emmett had got himself up onto the common, and there was no knowing how he would get down. He'd stand for a bit on his stick, she thought, let time pass on the sand by the oak tree. She would have helped him to get back down—on another day— or offered to walk with him, but she thought of the thigh and closed her eyes and walked on.

"I've got nothing left," he shouted after her. Lizzie heard him, and felt a trembling in her legs. She broke into a run and kept going. She wouldn't come up here again. That was the way to manage the encounter. She could leave him up here, and she wouldn't come this way again.

⚎

70. Having ventured out, open the front door to the house carefully. It will seem strange coming back in. It might seem a bit like a lair. You will long for something else, something cleaner, shinier, and a lot more anonymous. Like a hotel room, for example. Flat, crisp sheets. Scented puffy pillows. For the moment, this is where you live and work.

71. Place the keys in the small chipped bowl beside the front door, and collect any post from the mat. Remember, life will still be going on as normal out there. The post will still come to the house, and the postman will arrive in his red van at eleven in the morning, Monday to Saturday, still leave the engine running while he trots to the front door. The bills will come. They'll have to be paid. Everything can be done online.

72. Plant feet in slippers. Kick draft excluder into place.

73. Once in, look around. Is the house warm? Does it contain you for the moment? Are there not logs you can use to make a fire? Make a fire now. Put the

kettle on. Try to keep doing these things. You need
your body to help you through this. Keep it warm,
fed, contained, soothed. It needs to eat, digest, and
get you through this. Don't let it let you down.

Inside, there were soaps in the cupboard under the
stairs. Value packs, multiple Doves piled on the shelf.
With the Hoover that hadn't broken yet. And the old
ice-cream carton of clothes pegs that she'd spilled across
the kitchen table to choose one for her nose. And the
spare scrubbing brush. Once a year it was changed. Silly
objects she'd picked up on her shopping trips, to try to
furnish and feather things; and the cooking utensils and
the food was hers. And the small ceramic geese on the
sill that she'd hand-painted. Things were cleaned but
they always got dusty again with the dirt that came in
from the woods as he walked in and out from the driveway and from the car. In the beginning, it was him who'd
brought in all the dirt. He'd never been careful with the
doors, never seen her efforts to wash the floor. Then
she'd mentioned it to him and he had tried very hard to
wipe his shoes and keep the floors clean. He'd taken it
on as his job and done it very well. Which had made him
a good man—a kind man—and good enough to marry
at the Guildford registry office. He'd said they would
probably have kids in time. Tim Smith had come. Lizzie's
mother had come up from Hove. Jacob had given her a
sculpture of his hand as a wedding present. Then they'd

gone to the Italian restaurant in Guildford. That had been wonderful. A really special day.

No one would have thought, back then, that they'd end up in business together. She thought of the red lipstick and the red jumper and white skirt she'd been wearing on the wedding day. A white pencil skirt to the knee. It had been fabulous. Holding up a glass of champagne. With a little white beret and a rose pinned to the side of her head.

Twenty-five years later she'd tried to leave him. The summer before that he'd tried to leave her. He'd got as far as the Dog and Duck where he'd had some supper and taken a room for the night.

She'd got as far as the Cornstack Inn at Elstead. It had been a warm August evening and she'd driven with the windows open, smelling the heat in the fields.

She'd parked the Volvo on the green, outside the pub, and taken the only room that was available. Sixty quid for bed and breakfast. A pale room. Smooth sheets.

She'd slept well and woken knowing she was going to keep going.

They'd talked about a holiday to Spain, and she'd hoped they might have gone by now. It hadn't happened, but if she went back home after breakfast and opened up the laptop, she'd be able to book the trip with the savings she had in her own account. She would do it, she'd decided, straight after breakfast. Just for her. She had yogurt and fruit and coffee in the dining room. She paid the bill, dropped her napkin on the table and decided to book the flight. Going back home seemed a bit better then. There wouldn't be need for discussion, or any sort of disappointment if he'd changed his mind about the holiday because of her being a bad girl and leaving, or trying to leave.

She'd sat in the dining room looking out of the window at the bright patch of village green gone a little brown and dry after the summer. Then she'd driven the five miles home and gone straight through to the kitchen. She'd seen the dog stretching on her bed by the wall, yawning with a yelp to see her, white as fish, coming back in.

He'd come down much later than usual, as if he'd been waiting upstairs in bed for the sound of her car. Saturday morning. He'd said nothing, not even that he'd overslept or had trouble dropping off in the night. He'd stood at the sink eating a bun and watched the garden. The backs of his legs were tanned, freckled, and covered in that blondish down. He'd been talking about planting some trees; oak, he wanted, though the woods were mostly alder. He'd surprised her by asking about Spain then, and whether she still wanted to go.

"I'm going to go by myself," she'd said, in her coat still, her bag on the table. Tension had settled into her body over the years as they'd argued. A sort of survival tension: every nerve tight and ready to spring.

"That's such a shame," he'd said. "Because I'd like to go walking in Ronda with you."

74. Refrain from eating all day so that you will be hungry. Focus on that hunger in order to let it win out over the feeling of disgust that will come up as you lay the table for another meal.
75. When you get out of here, you will be entirely independent and can choose to live exactly as you please. You might choose never to eat at a table again. You might choose not to use a knife and fork to eat, let alone have such things in your possession.
76. You could simply go to a shop and buy a bag of carrots and eat them outside, standing on the street.
77. Think of that bag of carrots.
78. Think of that street in Scotland. And you standing on it—free—with a bag of carrots.
79. Pour yourself a large glass of wine.

6

The job wasn't so important as keeping the mind open to options and believing there were some. Even if she didn't get the job—it wasn't likely, given her appearance, and general demeanor, given what she'd done—she must carry on as normal, and press on with what life had in store for her this month.

The day dawned dry and calm. There wasn't to be an excuse in the weather. She lay in bed feeling enormous and achy and she placed her hands on her waist and felt around her hips and thighs. It was all there already, all that meat and fat.

Lynn, who managed the Bird Hotel on the outskirts of Farnham, was a large-breasted tall woman in navy sweatshirt, tailored trousers, and trainers. She had with her Steven, who'd worked before in video and visual communications in Farnham and held his hand out round a clipboard. They needed a team member, someone who would smile at the desk.

"Not much of a commute then," they said in unison, then beamed at each other and laughed. Lynn was probably in her early fifties too—but she was bouncy, and looked like the sort of woman who kept herself young by plugging in to a younger crowd.

In front of the sliding doors at the entrance, where they'd come to greet her, Lizzie looked down at her shoes. They looked small and dusty-black against her bobbly, woolly tights. The dog had come with her, and was chained up, whining, while traffic thundered past.

The hotel had one hundred and fifty rooms. The car park was being redesigned, which was why the Porta-kabin and tarpaulin were out there. The carpet was lilac and blue and green stripes, thin stripes. It was warm inside, and spacious.

Lynn took them to the circle of tub chairs in the lobby and went off to get some coffee. Steven's task was to make Lizzie feel relaxed, so he leaned back in the chair, stretched his legs out, smiled, and crossed his ankles. He pointed to the surveillance camera in the corner. They were putting new ones up in the car park, he said.

"You'll probably miss them, though," he said, grinning, and Lizzie wasn't sure what he meant. She felt herself retreating.

Then Steven said, "Precisely," with a finger up in the air, and she wondered what she'd missed in the conversation.

Lizzie chewed the inside of her cheek and felt the sweat slide in beads over her ribs. Her Wellingtons were in the bag beside her chair.

She lifted her chin to smooth out the saggy bit in her neck. She was still feeling sick.

Lynn came back with a tray of coffee and biscuits, and unwrapped the cling film. The biscuits were chocolate ones, cookies half dipped in chocolate. She pushed the plate over and then sat back in the tub.

"You've been out of work for a while," she said.

"Seven years," said Lizzie. Then she made a point of smiling at them both.

"And how do you feel?"

"I...?"

"How do you feel about having been out of work for seven years?" Lynn was smiling with her whole face. Her lips were softly crinkled at the corners, her eyes barely there.

Lizzie swallowed. "I feel nervous," she said. She let some air out through a small circle in her lips.

Steven nodded and wrote something down.

"Is that your dog out there?" said Lynn.

"Yes," said Lizzie. "Do you like dogs?"

"I do," said Lynn.

Lizzie closed her eyes, very briefly, and saw in her mind the steel-gray eyes she had loved, and then the stomach contents lain out on the grass.

"So, you've been busy making...cakes?"

"It's a hobby really. Yes."

"On your own?"

Lizzie said: "Yes. I'm newly alone."

"Me too," said Lynn, and then she bit down on a biscuit and gave Lizzie a cozy little wink.

Lizzie felt herself going a little pale. The stomach had been the only thing she had not been able to save. She had cut through the waist with the carving knife and managed to puncture it so that its contents slipped out onto the grass. She hadn't expected to see the meat lumps, and the actual oats. She'd expected to gag, but not like that, not from what had felt like her soul.

"How do you find it so far?" said Lynn. "Living on your own."

"I think I'll get used to it."

"I was ambivalent at first," said Lynn. She brushed some crumbs from her chest. "But now it's fine. Matter of fact, it suits me well."

Steven was looking embarrassed, looking down the length of his long legs at his shoes. Lizzie liked the fact that she could see that in him, when he was animated, when he was bored. She felt she'd not had this skill in the past. Being able to tell how others felt wasn't something that people without imagination were good at, Jacob had pointed out. She could see now that it wasn't true, that empathy was as much with her as it was with anyone. She smiled at Steven. He smiled back.

"I think it's all fine," said Lynn, looking, shrugging, at Steven. "Don't really see the point in our sitting here asking you all kinds of questions which aren't really relevant to whether you're going to be doing this job, and how. We've had a run of young ones and they've got restless and bored. Need someone who doesn't mind routine, who wants the job, you know?" She looked at Steven. "Yvonne wanted to travel and Vicky just sat here at the desk looking at the clock all day and reading her Facebook page. The hotel's not so busy in the week. We do conferences and weddings at the weekends. We need someone solid, reliable. And it seems to me that the best thing to do is just offer you the chance to come in for a few days sometime. We're doing refurbs. So it won't be till May."

She looked at Steven. "Sound all right?"

"Fine by me," said Steven, and he smacked his thigh quite gently with his fist. He'd drunk his coffee and seemed to be enjoying himself. "Thing is, it's a jungle out there," he went on, pointing a long white finger in the direction of the sliding doors and the main road.

Lizzie looked at him.

He looked back at her, and smiled. "Ah," he said. "I thought that would surprise you." He winked then, and Lizzie felt sure he'd started to tease. She didn't mind it though. She almost felt like she could tease back.

"Carrie will be working with you on the desk," said Lynn. "She's got a dog. She lives in Farnham with her Steven."

"Not me," said Steven. "He's a 'ph,' I believe." Then he spelled it out for her. Lizzie smiled. In ordinary circumstances she might well have found by now that she was having difficulty breathing. She looked at the light coming through the high windows and imagined herself in a church with some silent people sitting in the pews. Out on the main road life was hurtling by. Down in the woods there was a Volvo parked by her house with her husband's smell trapped in the upholstery. There was a freezer full of pieces of him. In here, though, up at the hotel, she was all right; and even though her heart was thumping underneath her interview shirt, she was quite safe, and the temperature was just right.

"Do you have a bike?" asked Steven, grinning as he bit into his biscuit.

Lizzie looked at the two of them.

"Steven comes by bike," said Lynn. "Like most people these days. Which is nice, isn't it? My son works in a bike shop in Farnham. Been there seven years now. Went to university and studied engineering. Ended up working in a bike shop. Quite happy, though. Loves it."

"Same with my mate Tom," said Steven. "He works at the garden center now. Studied for a degree in biology or something, I think. But you know that because he put us in touch with you, Lizzie. Said his neighbor was out of work and looking for a job."

"Yes. I know the neighbors," she said quietly.

"Tom's become a nice-looking young man," said Steven to Lynn in a way that made him sound like an uncle. "He didn't finish the degree."

"It was horticulture and garden design," said Lizzie.

"He didn't finish," said Steven.

"So working at the garden center to get some experience isn't such a bad idea," Lynn said.

"Yes, I know him," Lizzie said, leaning forward. She wasn't going to take the job. She was hot sitting here with the clot of anxiety in her chest. In a fortnight, or less, she'd be on a train to Scotland.

If she hadn't married a man like the one she did, she might have made better friends. She took a sip of her coffee. People leaned into life when it felt safe to do so. When life felt warm and inviting people came in to be there. Otherwise they hung back, waiting, growing pale. Had things been different, she might have gone up to the farm more regularly. Barbara was an odd woman, but she might have become a friend.

"Good coffee, isn't it?" said Lynn, resting her cup on her breast. She used her free hand to wipe around her face as if it were a flannel. Then she let out a huge sigh, as if, in almost offering Lizzie the job, she'd tired herself out. "Busy morning we've had so far, haven't we, Steven?"

"Very," he said, and nodded vigorously. Lizzie looked at their trainers. They were wearing the same ones: shiny white with a pale blue stripe running down the side.

"Is there a uniform?" she asked.

Lynn tilted her head over towards the reception desk where a girl was sitting with a headset on.

"Carrie's in," said Lynn. "See the shirt?"

Lizzie looked. It was a white shirt, with a soft frilly collar.

"What are the hours?" she said. Steven checked his clipboard.

"Varies," he said. "It's done on a rota. Eight-hour standard, though. Six till two. Eight till four. Ten till six. And so on."

"Well," said Lynn. "Not really 'so on.' We don't go beyond two in the afternoon till ten at night."

"No," said Steven.

They wondered if she'd like to have a think.

"How about we speak again Monday week?" he said.

Lizzie looked at them both and frowned. She was almost being offered a job. They stood up. Lizzie put her coffee cup down on the table and gathered her things.

"I'll show you over to the desk," said Lynn, "and you can meet Carrie."

80. You are well in there and on your way. It's time to take a little breather, and understand that there is no going back. Check into the body, and see how it is feeling.

81. Your husband's flesh will now be in your mouth and esophagus, your gullet, stomach and intestines.

82. If you have managed to go to the loo yet, he will

have also come out already as waste. Take a pause here. The more you take in, emotionally, at this point, the cleaner your bill of health is likely to be in the future.

83. Look at the poo.
84. What you have done this weekend is remarkable.
85. Don't suppress. If you need to run into the woods and scream into the trunk of a tree, then do that. Once. Do it. Do it quickly. Move on.

It *was* remarkable. On Sunday morning, she'd cooked the right foot. With pumpkin. She ate at the table using the fruit knife to take strips off the bone. She sat perfectly still and upright, not needing to read the newspaper or listen to the radio. The workings of her mouth, brain and jaw had been in perfect unison. No need for thought. Open. Close. Chew. Swallow. Then the toenails, the knuckles and the smaller bones had been crushed in a blender with salt, turmeric and cumin. She'd eaten the mush heaped on a plate with herbs from the garden; she had all sorts, and rosemary gave it character. The ankle she put in the stockpot and reduced, as before. Then blended again. Reduced, reduced. Then she'd put the stock in a Tupperware container in the fridge.

At the Dog and Duck on the way back from the hotel, Lizzie ordered a glass of white wine and a packet of crisps. Mike, behind the bar, had a ponytail of dreadlocked hair and a black ring in his eyebrow. He said there was a bowl round the back, by the door to the garden, if Rita needed a drink.

"It's OK," Lizzie said, catching sight of her face in the mirror behind the bar. Despite her efforts at makeup—enough to cover the marks and sags—she still looked pale. "What a fright," she whispered, as her mother would have done, fingering the coins in her purse.

"It's not busy," he said. "For a Monday."

Lizzie gave him a five-pound note. Already this morning she had spoken more words than she'd usually done in a week. It wasn't hard to find a few more.

"Was it busy at the weekend?"

"Had a guitarist here Saturday night. He was all right. Old Emmett from the farm got stuck at that table in the corner. Had to give him a fireman's lift to the car and take him home."

Lizzie thought of the stick and the barrel chest and the wave of white hair. It would be hard to lift him onto a shoulder. Even a strong shoulder like Mike's. A year ago there had been a MISSING poster on a tree in the lane with a photograph of Emmett. It had been up high on the trunk, but Jacob reckoned the old man had pinned the poster to the tree himself. "Has to be him. Who else?" he'd said. In the picture Emmett had been younger than he was by about a decade, smiling into the camera with eyes that had been whited out by Tipp-Ex.

"You all right with that lot? Need a tray?"

Lizzie shook her head and grinned at Mike and then carried her wine and crisps out to the garden. There were ducks on the wet grass and the leaves from a weeping willow clogged up the surface of the stream. It was almost sunny. Lizzie sat on a bench at one of the wooden tables, using her mac to keep her bottom dry. She took little puffs on a cigarette. Emmett should have been put in a home by now. He wasn't a danger to others, or to himself; he wasn't someone who should be isolated from the community, but he wasn't right. He was old and his mind had gone. They should have taken him in, she reflected. She took a deep puff and tried to lift her shoulders. She hadn't smoked much in the last twenty years, but she always enjoyed it when she did. She and Jacob had tried to give up, as a couple, a number of times. Whoever had given in first had been bashful, relieved, defiant out in the garden.

He'd smoked with his left hand, holding the tip right up close to his palm like a good-looking actor he'd seen in a film. She'd barbecued that left hand on Sunday evening in a treacle marinade, wrapped it in foil and let it cook for twenty-five minutes only. She'd broken it up while it was still in the foil with the carving knife, and she'd been able to suck the meat, which was wet around the wrist and the fatty bit above the thumb. Jacob had told her that a quarter of the brain's motor cortex was devoted to working the muscles of the hand. At the kitchen table, with a glass of wine, and the radio on, she'd tasted blood and skin and winced into a forkful of fluffy mashed potato, and she'd crunched the ice-cool slices of cucumber carefully, and spooned on a little minted yogurt. She'd started flossing again now, too.

Now she teased her hair a bit with her smoking hand. She looked at her nails. It was possible that she'd been offered a job. Determination. As if she were missing a piece, he'd said. "Ego, Lizzie, and determination, to do things for yourself." Two fat ducks scrambled out of the water and waddled towards where she was sitting hunched on the edge of the bench. They stopped a few feet away, and then put their beaks to the ground. But she could do things for herself. Good or bad, she'd always, in a sense, been doing things for herself.

Emmett had come to the barbecue they'd had once— the only social occasion—and he'd done nothing but sit forward on one of the chairs, staring into the trees. He was mad and old and decrepit, and he did nothing, and that gave him time to smell the air and notice things. Of all the people around here, he was the one she feared most.

She took the glass back inside and put it on the edge of the bar so that Mike wouldn't have to wade outside in the watery grass to get to it.

"Cold out," he said, and then he began to whistle as he took the glass through to the kitchen. He came back to the bar with a packet of cigarettes. "Here," he said.

"Someone left a pack on the bar last night. I've given up, my girlfriend hates it. If you take them, you'll be doing me a favor."

86. You may feel that nothing is the same as it was be-fore your husband died. There may be a strange feeling of stillness, as if everything is on pause. It may seem that the old thoughts and preoccupations have gone away. You may feel as if you are looking at the world through a different person's eyes. Is there a new sense of light? Is there humor? Kind-ness?

87. Write down your name. If you want to. And your age. Don't bother if it doesn't make sense to you. Write down a few things that you like.

Coming home, walking up the steps with the ache of tiredness in her legs and her shoes in a plastic bag, Lizzie saw the ceramic bowl on the sill that he'd put there for loose change. And a book his mother had given him for addresses and telephone numbers. He'd not had friends. He'd explained that it wasn't clear to him the exact reason why. He'd made a few at the prep school he'd been sent to, and then some at the boys' public school in the Midlands. Sporty place, he'd said, drawing on a cigarette, and she'd seen something then in the tension around his eyes. She'd felt that she understood his isolation.

"Were you always going to be an artist?" Lizzie asked him once, after they'd managed sex and were lying together in his room listening to the sound of the rain. She'd been at the house for months; he hadn't tried to sculpt a thing. The cast was off his leg, but the three bags of clay were still in the shed. He had brought in a huge branch from the woods, and she had teased him about that. They'd put it on the kitchen floor. She had taken photographs and felt like the kooky girl in the weird tights. Jacob had been at ease, his face looking young and calm. Lizzie had taken the tights off. He'd gone to get the wine. She hadn't had much sex in her life—a few unmemorable encounters at art school, and the virginity she'd lost on the beach at sixteen. She'd been very surprised, in the kitchen with him, by how much she'd enjoyed the feelings in her body. Then they'd gone upstairs and done it again, slowly this time, while looking at each other.

Lizzie hadn't known if Jacob was any good at sculpture. Certainly she'd not been able to say anything to him about his work. No wonder he'd skipped about on Joanna's encouragement. Joanna thought he was curious, that his work was "moving." At her house in London she would have said so.

"I just need to go to the shed. I need to do something," he'd say.

"Now?"

"Yes."

"It's after dark. It's dinnertime."

He'd reach for the wine and agree that she had a point.

"I can go after dinner. That's what I'll do."

"Yes, that's an idea."

Somehow the two of them were sucking up all the air.

In the afternoon, she stood in the garden in her boots and coat and looked at the lawn. It had rained in the night. Not a great downpour, and certainly not the deluge she'd hoped for on the first day when the blood and clots had been about. She looked over to the spot where his body had been. There wasn't much to see now, apart from a brownish stain by the hole he'd been digging. The sun had gone in.

Still in her black interview suit with her skirt stiff around her knees, she took the spade from its hook on the back of the shed door. She put her foot against the blade and began to pull the turf up. She heard the high shriek of a bird in the trees behind her and felt the air on her cheeks. The tears were there and that was a relief. Under the anxiety was a person trying to get on. There wasn't much one could do with devastation but try to find a thread of hope. There was hope of getting through this and to a small room in Scotland. She drove the spade into the grass with her foot and the dog ran around, sniffing the soil.

88. Have you thought about the axe and spade? Is there somewhere nearby where you might like to bury them?
89. You could dig a big hole in the flower bed and put them there.
90. Or drop them off at the dump?
91. Or leave them at the garden center, perhaps. What about out round the back where the pots are. You could slide them under one of those giant trolleys on which they stack the pots. Who would notice? Wouldn't they just be there, gathering dust and spiders, for months?

Overnight, his right lower leg and knee had been out on the kitchen windowsill in its bag. Lying stiff with the cover tucked around her in bed on Tuesday morning, Lizzie thought about what might have come in the night and sniffed it. She would be cutting away the tender flesh from the calf, which could be eaten as fillet, with brown rice and vegetables. It would be plump, and cut in two, the size of chicken breasts.

She didn't know what she'd be doing with the rest of

the leg. After the calf she would have only the long central bone and the knee, neither of which could be eaten easily.

In the shower she washed her hair and then stood hunched on the mat and rubbed it dry. She caught sight of her white shoulders in the mirror and chose not to look up from there or down at the sagging breasts. Dry and dressed, she came downstairs, stepping tentatively into the kitchen with Jacob's shaving cream and razor in hand and had a quick glance around. She put the tools on a tray, and made herself a coffee with milk. She filled a glass mixing bowl with hot water. In the garage, she put the lights on. She took the left lower leg and knee piece out of the freezer and left it to defrost in its bag on the lid. Then she knelt down beside the bin liner, using one of the cushions from the garden chairs to rest her knees; and she punctured the bin liner with a knife, ripping the plastic open.

Keeping it steady on the plastic, Lizzie shaved his right leg, rinsing the razor after each stroke in the glass bowl. She worked slowly. She'd got used to careful preparation. It was going to take most of the afternoon. The joint was cold but had thawed nicely. She put her hand on the wound. In her mind she saw the leg in shorts, or white under his dressing gown and creaking up the stairs at bedtime. She held on to the kneecap, and moved it a little beneath her hand. She lifted the leg in its bin liner and went through to the kitchen.

The meat came away easily from the back of the leg. She rinsed it at the sink, cut it into two fillets, and then laid them in a baking tray with olive oil, black pepper and salt. The leg meat went into the oven for half an hour, just as it was.

Out on the patio the barbecue was cleaned up and ready. Carrying the remainder of his lower right leg and knee under her arm, she went to the shed for the axe, then put the leg on the ground and made a clean break through the smooth-shaven shin. Now it was in two manageable pieces, each a bit longer than her own hand. Lizzie wrapped them securely in foil, and then lifted the pieces onto the barbecue. They nestled in among the coals. Black pepper, she thought. And lemon juice.

She'd found there was a rhythm to this. She was settling in. It was nearly spring. She got some wood from the garage to make a bonfire on the lawn.

Outside, the dog ran around in the near darkness while Lizzie stood in the kitchen and watched.

She went upstairs to the linen cupboard. She had eaten the tender fillets from the back of his leg, plain, on a plate at the table. She was keeping busy while she digested. The rest of the lower right leg was cooling in its foil parcels on the shelf beside the barbecue. Rita sniffed the meat, then turned and whined, then ran back to sniff some more.

The towels were to go on the bonfire, and all the

sheets. There were three spare duvet covers, including the one he'd given her as a present, with the flowers on. This one she threw into the bedroom on her way down the stairs. The rest went out with her through the back door and onto the pile in the garden.

She looked at the lawn of brown muddy holes from her turfing job, and the bonfire right in the middle with the old towels and the white crumpled sheets.

Everything from the drawer full of paper clips and batteries, old receipts and other clobber went in the bin. She was left with an almost empty drawer containing a china bowl of various stationery items including the old stapler Jacob had sworn they'd lost years before. She also found the Sellotape.

She spritzed everything in the kitchen in a lemon-scented spray and wiped it all down, using cloths that were warm and thick and full of hot soapy water.

She lit a candle, put the heating on, and went out to the barbecue for the leg bone and the knee.

7

His books and all the Christmas decorations went on the bonfire. Lizzie carried the books in her arms and put them on top of the sheets and towels. His alarm clock went on. And a book he'd been reading about Spain. In his bedside drawer there were tissues, a tin bowl of badges, old foreign coins. And a bleary photograph of her in a frame. She wasn't smiling, but looking absent, in a woolen hat, on a walk.

Everything went on the bonfire apart from the tin bowl and the badges and coins, which she dropped into the recycling box by the back door.

She hurried down with his clothes and got the warm, awful fug of him on the stairs.

The bedside table went on too. And the white paper lining.

It was easier, she thought, flying back up, to just put everything on. There'd be nothing left in the house. She'd be clearing out, ready to start again.

She came back down the stairs two at a time, and stopped for a drink in the kitchen. Her heart was pounding. The right lower leg bits were still on the table, still on her plate. She wasn't eating. She was too busy. It was night. There wasn't time. In the garage there was petrol. She poured it on his jumper, on the pillows. It went like this at night. A little drink, and then a binge. Lots to do. Things leaped forward. A midnight conflagration. Poor people in the village, she thought, shaking the can onto the pile. She was back in her Wellies. If they ever knew. She thought about Joanna outside the antiques shop with him. Her mother would have called it an affair. Plain and simple. It didn't matter what they actually did with each other. He had felt it; she had felt it. That was an affair.

She rolled up the *Farnham Herald* and made a flaming torch. She threw it towards the bonfire, but from too far away, so she tried again, going closer this time, and the torch met the fuel on the pillows and burst into flame.

Lizzie walked into the kitchen with her arms folded, and she sat down at the table with a knife and fork. She crunched and ate the lower right, sitting upright as she had been taught to do as a child, using a napkin to dab at the corners of her mouth. She sat there for two and a half hours, still in her boots. She chewed around the knee by lifting the leg with both of her hands to her mouth. Her teeth went into his flesh and pulled it away. It was dark outside, everything was quiet but the dog moving around the bonfire, restless, jumping, coming back into the kitchen, trying to be still.

She looked at the clock. It was 2 a.m.

*   *   *

His left lower leg was also pale. In the garage she sat cross-legged in thick socks to shave it and prepare it with olive oil and salt. Her heart was still pounding. She leaned over it, trying not to voice her thoughts. She could feel the jutting in her jaw and the aching in her neck and shoulders. Her stomach was huge now, and she felt like a spider with a sack of him in her belly.

This time she didn't chop the leg into two pieces with the axe. It was still cool but had thawed. She ran her hand along the smooth shin and then rolled it carefully in tin foil. She slipped her feet back into her boots and then carried it under her arm to the bonfire.

It went in on his books. She waited, for half an hour. It was 4 a.m. She'd brought the duvet down from upstairs and had bundled up in it to drink coffee laced with sherry. It was warm and comforting. Sparks from the bonfire were flying out into the garden. She walked around on the grass.

Joanna had come here once. Lizzie remembered how they had sat, the three of them, in the garden, eating cake. It had been a warm summer's day, and Lizzie had felt moldy beside the pale gray of Joanna's shirt and the tailoring of her trousers. She had told Joanna that she'd been raised by a single mother and knew that a woman had to work to get anywhere in the world. She'd learned about life from sitting behind the counter in the

Becketts' shop as a child, and she knew what commerce meant. Something had diverted her, she'd said, high on a drink. Something had thrown her off.

Joanna hadn't come again. Not to the drip of the ugly trees. So damp and dreary, she'd say to her friends, if she told them at all. Or perhaps she'd kept her country visit a secret. Perhaps she'd simply woken up the next morning and jumped out of bed, feeling it slip out of her memory without having to think about pushing it out at all. Jacob and Lizzie Prain. Why would anyone remember them?

Jacob had come upstairs after Joanna had gone. He'd done nothing but lie down beside her in his clothes and put an arm around her. She'd felt needed then. He'd hoped Joanna was going to commission a sculpture. She hadn't done. But he still had his Lizzie, and in his own private battle with what he was trying to do he'd needed to know, she felt, that they still had each other, and their little life under the trees wasn't a fantasy of Joanna's, or his, but a real life, simple and ordinary: soap and bread, and a dog that would need a walk in the morning.

She unhooked the barbecue tongs from the hooks nailed into the wooden slats on the side, and she pushed the leg about in the embers of the bonfire.

The sad fallacy of disguising with flavors was beginning to exhaust her, so this time she simply used her gloved hands to smooth out the hot foil on the table outside, and she sat down in her duvet, the torch now dead, the lights on in the kitchen.

With knife and fork she ate it, in small bits. It was past five in the morning, and the wine was gone.

Lizzie went to the bottom of the garden and stood for a long time by the shed, in the dark, her hand on the window ledge. She looked at the moon above the trees and straightened her back. She had put the bone on the dying fire. She stared around the garden, then up at the moon again. All around, the trees were slowly taking on light and color. She felt the cold. She should have put all of him on the fire instead of eating him. She could have been standing there for one night only, with a glass of wine and a packet of cigarettes, watching the bonfire rage through the night, standing to one side, detached: how some people got through divorce.

92. Eating him might turn out to be kinder.
93. We won't call it an "act of love" as such. But you are doing it with care and attention. You will get nourishment and strength, and a sense of achievement. Completion. A job done.
94. Hope is a quiet room in Scotland.
95. You are doing the best you can.

*   *   *

Lizzie pushed against the shed door and went into the small space at the front. She stood for a moment in the dust. Right in front of her, keeping quiet in the moonlight, was a wall of junk, of boxes and television aerials, old picture frames, a cardboard box with a saucepan handle and a ladle, and a pile of newspapers he'd been keeping. There was an old kettle, another frame with cracked glass, paint cans, bundles of tarpaulin, an old casserole dish, and a box of his records. At her feet, the penis sculpture Joanna hadn't wanted. He'd come back with that one; he'd flushed red in the kitchen and said, "Oh well." He'd missed her by miles.

🍴

96. This isn't the time for oughts and shoulds.
97. Have the courage to go mad completely if that's what it takes. Just let yourself feel whatever comes up as you go along.
98. Don't take the thoughts or the feelings seriously. You're passing through time. That's all this is.

"Lizzie," she said, "go to bed," but when she lay down upstairs in the coat and the duvet her stomach heaved and her head spun with all that she'd had to drink. She went back downstairs and walked around the garden. Then she went for a shower and washed her hair.

She wrote a note for the postman with instructions to put the post in the box attached to the hawthorn. Outside it was bright and cold.

She heard the shushing of wheels in the lane and turned. Her legs were heavy and her face was tight and dry. Mike from the pub was on his bike, tall and broad-chested, in a faded blue sweatshirt. His dreadlocks were pinned back from his face. She stared at the ring in his eyebrow and the mud on his chin.

In her time here she'd not met many people in the lane.

"Nice hat," he said, pointing to the beret she'd found in the shed. It was the hat she'd worn on her wedding day. She felt very far away. She was tired and confused.

"Good timing," he said. "I was coming to find you."

"I haven't slept," she mumbled, but he didn't seem to hear. He looked back up the lane the way he'd come. Sunlight was piercing the trees. She followed his gaze, her eyes narrowing to slits. In her mind she saw posters pinned to the bark.

"Guess what?" he said, as if he'd known her a really long time.

She turned to look at him and felt her heart beating through her coat. Her scalp itched under the beret.

"Thank you for the cigarettes," she said, before he could speak. She wasn't sure what he knew of her and her husband. He had worked at the pub for nearly five years. "I'm getting hitched," he said. "I'm going to propose to her in the pub. Tonight."

Lizzie looked where he'd looked, where he was pointing, back up the lane. There wasn't much to see, apart from the hawthorns, and the dripping alders. A load of sand from the verge had slipped into the road further up, making a yellowy muddy slick on the side. When the twins had gone to secondary school Emmett had put a MISSING poster of them as toddlers up on the telegraph pole. Jacob had found that funny.

"Nic," said Mike, grinning, leaning back on his bike.

"I'm going to ask her to marry me," he said. "You know Nic. Up at the farm? Plaits. Colorful hats. We've been going out two years. She works in a shop."

Lizzie nodded.

"Jewelry's her main thing. She makes it."

Lizzie nodded, remembering the girls who ran a stall one year outside the Dog and Duck. Everything tiny, labeled, penciled in, immaculate. Two stick-thin girls and their vast parents propping up the background like a painted man and woman you put your head through at the seaside.

"They ran a stall," she said. "When they were young. About fourteen."

Mike laughed and rolled forward on his handlebars.

"That's when she got this thing about making jewelry."

"I know Tom, their brother," she blurted. "He sold me a barbecue at the garden center. He showed me how to use it."

"Tom's a nice guy," Mike said. "Bit misunderstood, I think. Anyway, time to change all that. Time to bring a little love into that household. Then focus on the career."

"What are you going to do?" said Lizzie, hearing not her own voice but someone else's. Another voice from round here. Not hers.

"I'm going to teach," he said, holding a hand out to the woods as if there were children in there.

Lizzie smiled. She liked thinking about Tom Vickory in his own little world, moving around everyone else up at the farm. Misunderstood. She didn't know why it made her feel happy to hear that. She had an image of him as a little boy in her mind. She'd been to the garden center so many times in the last year. She'd hung around and watched him work. It had been a place to go to, a place to get away. There was another garden center halfway up the A3 that she'd been to once with Jacob. Driving round the car park, looking for somewhere to park.

"It's Nic's birthday," Mike said. "Don't suppose—long shot—you can make a cake?"

Lizzie looked at his face, and the easy, wide-open smile of a man for whom life had not been particularly complicated. She could see it with these two, how the troubled girl from up the road would come to depend on the easygoing lad with the dreadlocks and ring in his brow. She'd let herself be folded in these arms. They'd be looking for a place to live. They'd have a family of their own. The girl would be breaking away now from her life at the farm.

"Yes," she said, thinking of the beret on her head. Her new, fresh start. In the shed she'd brushed it and whacked it to get the dust off. "Yes, I can make a cake."

It was a tiny act of faith.

Jacob had said, after he'd been to London once, "We've got to learn to swim upstream, Lizzie."

Joanna had taught him how to try to make a life on little acts of faith. One after the other. Even if there wasn't a baby. Or a career path.

"We still have to live as *if*, Lizzie," he'd said, raising his hands to her. "Otherwise we are swimming in a vortex and life has no meaning."

She hadn't known how to reply, and she hadn't really understood what he meant by a vortex with water in it. He had always come back like that: all uppity and full of bright ideas. He'd bounced around like a pup for a few days. And she'd not known how to be. Not knowing what she was feeling about his trips to London, she'd gone around saying nothing. She'd gone to work and forgotten it. When she'd lost her job she'd not been able to do that. She'd got clumsy instead. The anger had come out sideways. All around her things had slipped, got broken or lost.

It was getting cold in the lane.

"I can do that. Yes," she said. "I can make a cake."

"Cool," he said. "My budget's forty-five quid. And she likes chocolate."

"Does she like anything else? I can do a chocolate cake but it needs to be in the shape of something."

"Shoes," he said, smiling.

Lizzie said, "Shoes." And she thought of some red ones with a high heel. She looked down and peered over her stomach at her big muddy boots. She'd worn awful shoes to the interview. It didn't matter. In Scotland she would buy anew.

"She's got so many shoes," said Mike, flexing the brakes with his fingers. He laughed.

"I'll bring it to the pub tonight," she said. "What time will she be there?"

"Midnight," he said, "knowing her. Though I said to get there round eight."

Lizzie thought of the black car pulling out of the farm. Dad driving, twins all thin and bright, Mum sitting squashed in the front, Emmett in the back, staring, tiny, out at the lane.

No one would love Lizzie Prain now.

Perhaps it didn't matter.

"Seven thirty?" she said.

"Yes," he said, "great!"

He held out a hand to shake. Lizzie looked at it and offered her own. In the warmth of his, her hand felt small and cold. She needed badly to sleep.

"Great," he said again.

Then he whipped the handlebars round and cycled away.

8

Lizzie watched him cycle up the lane towards Puttenham, and then she went back to the house.

It was freezing cold inside and she couldn't get warm. In the kitchen she wrote: *I can't do it anymore.* Then she tore the paper into small pieces and put each piece in her mouth. She let them melt on her tongue. She pushed her tongue through the pieces of paper. She swallowed them. The agent would say, about the kitchen and garage: "It's clean here, and simple. A good place to start." She made a cup of coffee, and went out into the sunlight.

Lizzie had been fifteen when her mother had dumped Ian Harper. He'd been a primary school teacher in Brighton. They'd run on the beach together at weekends. Afterwards Anne said that the only way to get over a man you loved was to imagine the pair of you in a car crash and him walking away in shock leaving you bleeding in the car.

Lizzie stood now with her cup of coffee and stared at the lawn and the ash patch where she'd burned almost everything in the last few days. She thought of Jacob walking away. He'd be looking down, she felt, at something in his hands. She could see herself, watching him, upside down in the crash. She wouldn't be feeling her own pain, but his lack of it: "Poor bugger can't feel," she'd be thinking, with blood pouring from her nose and into her hair. "Poor man can't handle his own feelings," she'd be thinking, first, and her heart, close to the gearstick, would be going out to him, to his back as he walked away.

99. Absolutely classic codependent thinking: catastrophizing, clinging on: anyone got some steroids they can punch into this self-esteem?

100. A good opportunity to come in here and try to encourage a little more focus on the body parts in the freezer?

"For God's sake, don't feel sorry for me," Anne had said when Lizzie was fifteen, and the two of them were sitting up at the table in the window of the boarding house in Hove.

The Becketts' was a good place to live, especially after some of the scum houses they'd been in when Lizzie was small. It was warm and clean and well lit, and they slept in a double bed beneath a huge pink eiderdown. Lizzie was by the wall, and Anne was next to the oversized wicker table so that she could reach for things in the night. The room had a high ceiling. It was extremely spacious, Lizzie told Jacob. A double room with sea views and a substantial bathroom. The room had been furnished with a bed, wooden table, wardrobe and two chairs. There had been a fireplace, but they didn't use it, because the house had central heating. There was a cast-iron radiator that their feet could touch if they poked them out of the end of the bed. They could also hang their socks, tights, pants and thermal vests on the radiator, which meant they were warm when they went in the morning to put them on. The wardrobe was French, she told Jacob, and the tallest part was level with her mother's ear. On the ledge above the fireplace they kept their hairbrushes and hair elastics. In the bathroom they kept their toothbrushes, toothpaste, shampoo and soap. They'd go and get books from the library, and cook downstairs in the Becketts' kitchen. Anne made good bread.

Anne did her chores in the house, and in the Becketts' shop, and Lizzie, as a small child, would watch her. On Fridays the whole house ate fish and chips on the promenade, and this was where Anne first met Ian. For a long time they kept one of the pictures he took with the camera. Late spring, and the photograph showed them soaking up the first rays of sun, squinting on the benches in front of the house. Mr. Beckett was in shorts and sandals, Mrs. B in her powder-blue dress, then Anne in a mustard-yellow roll-neck jumper. Then Lizzie, tall and frizzy, in a dress and cardigan, red tights, ankle boots.

Ian Harper was walking up the shingle beach towards them when he stopped to take their picture. He ended up taking a whole roll before Mr. Beckett went down there to ask what he was doing.

🍴

101. Think vegetarian thoughts. In case the meat is getting to you.
102. Nut rissoles remain popular. And goat's cheese phyllo parcels.
103. All those things you can do with pomegranate seeds and pine nuts.
104. You have all this to look forward to.
105. Ratatouille?
106. You probably won't feel like eating chicken ever again. No matter.

Jacob hadn't really been listening to the story. But she'd wanted to tell him—especially since he'd said there were things missing in her, about her childhood—and prove to him and to herself that she could remember it all.

She'd said: "Ian Harper didn't come that night. He didn't come the next night either. He turned up three days later. He had a large brown suitcase and that camera hanging round his neck. Like I have," she said, pointing to her own.

"He was wearing a crinkled light-colored suit, and a bowler hat. He was handsome, and he came in first to the shop on the ground floor. He said that he'd been to London. He apologized for not having let everyone know. He was polite and softly spoken. I liked him.

"He and Mum must have been the tallest pair on the south coast of England. We knew it wouldn't last. It didn't last. He was brokenhearted; she was impulsive.

" 'Disappointment is the main thing to get your head around, Lizzie,' she told me, Jacob. 'And really try not to drink,' she said."

"Nothing lasts," Jacob had said.

Lizzie had smiled, and nodded, and looked around her kitchen. Then she said how, even though her mother got so maudlin about it, she'd known that Anne was more interested in Ian Harper than she'd said she was.

"You just can't tell with love," Lizzie had said to her new husband. "When he came down to our room, she stopped moving jaggedly, with her lips collapsed and her chin pushing up, which was how she looked when she was concentrating and tired. When Ian came down she spoke more softly and tried to walk sexily around the room, like she was in a bikini and wading into the sea. He took her out to the pub at the end of the road, and she wore her flares and her see-through top and put rose oil on her wrists and behind her ears.

"They'd wander up and down the beach like a pair of wading birds, up the shingle, over the pelican crossing and into the Becketts' house. A few times we went out for fish and chips. Twice he took her out for dinner, which I picture as a somber and mournful affair, with both of them bending over a low pub table, her trying to help him with his sadness. Ian's wife had left him and gone to America, Mr. Beckett told me. Broke the bugger's heart in two, he said.

"Mum was pregnant when Ian Harper left, but she didn't expect him to come back so she had the pregnancy terminated. She'd been through enough by then. She was forty-one. She wasn't the kind of person who wanted to settle down, and we didn't have things. She liked to be in a position from which she could spring and run at once; and in the meantime, she needed a bed for the two of us, and somewhere to store our clothes.

"Another thing you don't know about my childhood, Jacob, is the fact that I had a job. I'd work for the Becketts in their shop at the weekends and sometimes in the afternoons. I liked doing the pricing, getting things ready for delivery, and weekend mornings were busy with locals coming in for staples. Then the holidaymakers buying nets and flags to take to the beach. It was cool in there, the best place to be, I thought.

"Mum found it deathly in the shop. She preferred working with Mrs. Beckett in the guest rooms, dragging rugs out into the air and beating them, flipping beds, driving the vacuum back and forth. So I sat at the counter when I was home from school, and I was quiet there, and diligent. I didn't read, or allow my thoughts to wander. I sat on the stool and waited for my customers. I liked being in the window, close to the sea. I sat and listened and watched. Which was how I got to hear about Ian and how he hadn't gone to work on an oil rig and he'd never had a wife. He was all anyone talked about for a little while. Who the hell was he? they said. Wasn't who he said he was. And it gave people the creeps now to think about his long, skinny body shambling round the town. So sweet, they said. Unassuming. Always are, they said, when they're on the run. Could be Irish, they said. Come here to keep hush. They talked about it right by the counter, and it didn't matter to me in the end because I learned that the story about Ian Harper and my mother gave the local people something to take their minds off things."

107. All sorts of interesting recipes can be found on the Internet.

108. A sweet pineapple marinade can be used on any cut of meat to give it a fresh, light, fruity lift. The one I'd like to suggest has a great Hawaiian teriyaki

flavor and will work beautifully with strips of meat laid over rice.

109. It takes all of six minutes to make and will give you about two cups of sauce.

110. Ingredients: 1 cup crushed pineapple. Absolutely fine to use the tins you've got in the cupboard.

> 1/3 cup soy sauce
> 1/3 cup honey
> 1/4 cup cider vinegar
> 2 cloves garlic, minced
> 1 teaspoon ginger powder
> 1/4 teaspoon powdered cloves
>
> Preparation: mix all the ingredients together and use immediately or store in an airtight container for up to seven days.

Lizzie's mother had come to the wedding and hung back, looking awkward in pastels. Once or twice she'd glanced at her daughter's stomach, just to check, Lizzie thought, for any accident that might have prompted the decision to wed this rather odd woodland-dwelling antiques man. Who had been charming on his wedding day. Open-armed and steering everyone about. As if, like Lizzie with the axe and saw that desperate Monday morning, he'd always known what to do.

*   *   *

At seven it was dark. She drove up to the pub in the car with the cake on the front seat. Mike was waiting for her, standing in the porch smoking a roll-up. He was wearing a red bow tie, and his dreadlocks were slicked back away from his face.

Lizzie stood in the porch and peeled back the tin foil. The shoes had come out really well. They were black and white striped.

"Man!" he said. Then he showed her how his hand was shaking. He blew on his hands and shifted his weight from one foot to the other.

Lizzie was quiet. It was dark in the porch, and cold. She looked at the shoes.

"I think they'll be fine," she said, feeling the heat coming off his body.

"They're really beautiful," he said.

Lizzie swallowed while she tried to find a response.

"It's time, you know?" he said, straightening his back and standing up tall in the porch. "It's just about bloody time. Me. And Nic. I love her. I'm nervous. It's OK. I'm not good enough, that's what I feel."

"I think the fact that you can say what you feel will be good enough for her. And good enough for anybody," Lizzie said, quietly.

He took the cake from her hands and took a deep, clearing breath.

"Are you going to do it in front of everyone, Mike?"

"Yup."

"Gosh."

"Nah, man. I'm ready. Ready as I'll ever be."

"Me too," she said. "I'm leaving here, I'm putting the house on the market."

"You're kidding! I love that little house. See it every time I go cycling past and think how much I love that place. A sweet little home. You know? Wish I could have one of my own. For me and Nic."

Lizzie tucked the foil back under the plate. Then she looked up at him and her eyes settled longingly on his soft young cheek.

"Perhaps you can," she said.

$$\text{\ding{45}}$$

111. Temptations will be everywhere. You will be drawn to young people. Young, happy people, especially those in love, will seem very attractive to you. You will be extremely sensitive to the smells coming off them. They will seem warm and musky and heaven to be around. You will find yourself leaning in with what feels like an innocent kind of love, a sense of wanting to be friends with them, but watch the old throbbing sensations, and the dreams you will be making. Summer afternoons with jugs of lemonade

and strong brown arms folding around you and drawing you close are the stuff of dreams only; in all probability not visions of a future for you.

112. This doesn't mean you won't be happy.

"I'll come tomorrow with the money," he said. She looked down at the heel on his cowboy boots. She'd taken her hair out of its clip. Now she tried to flick it back with a jerk of her head.

"Good luck," she said, "and let's speak again."

She took the steps two at a time, and quickly belted her swollen body into the car. Her stomach was gurgling and her insides felt very heavy now, as when she'd had too much dairy over a number of days. There was also a thick, oily feeling in her mouth, which made it hard to swallow. She sipped water, then put the bottle back into her coat pocket. She was getting sick. She would need to go home and have a cup of tea beside the fire.

She put her headlights on as she drove back up the lane, then flicked them down when she saw the car coming the other way. She knew it was her neighbors from up at the farm and she looked into the back of the car as it passed by to see if the old man was there.

By now she was trembling at the wheel. She made an effort to park the car very neatly, very precisely, half in, half out of the ditch, as it had always been.

She got out of the car and stood in the dark with

her hands the same lengths at the sides. She looked up through the trees and saw not a single star in the sky.

It was remarkable how people managed in life, how they got on without worrying too much about it, she thought.

"Get up and put your lipstick on," Anne had said, standing tall with her daughter, almost to the ceiling of the rented room in Hove. "Get up and brush your hair and wash and cream your face as if your life were not as it is but better."

Lizzie had asked her mother how you creamed your face as if your life were not as it was but better, and Anne had shown her how to do it slowly, and tenderly, with a look of pride, like someone would if they had all day to go and watch water voles swimming or play tennis with a friend.

"The thing to remember is: only you know how bad it is. Only we know what we know. Therefore only we see it like that. We have the power then to pretend it isn't, to smile as if we believe."

"Pretend until it's better" had been one of Anne's favorite sayings, and Lizzie, born in the dead of winter, 8 a.m. with a sea view, had learned early on that one had to be practical to get through.

Now she secured the head torch. Kneeling in the dark, she cut the bin liner and peeled it open. She spread the plastic out on the lawn, and looked. She had used the carving knife to slice under the rib cage and cut above the diaphragm. His chest had shoulders, but no arms attached: no head. She'd axed the upper arms, leaving the shoulders on, so that he looked like a Greek bust, with a splendid, prominent cage of ribs.

In the beam of the torch the torso looked very white. She'd been able to get down on the grass and look up through the cage to the heart and lungs. She'd had to bleed the chest with a clothes peg on her nose, by tilting it into the flower bed by the shed, and she'd worried, briefly, that the heart and lungs might slip out onto the grass. That hadn't happened, though. She bent forward on her knees and peered up into his ribs. All the red and purple bits were still in there.

113. As you work, various thoughts and feelings may come to the surface. These could be things as silly or trivial as, thank goodness he wasn't the kind of man to wear jewelry around his neck; or they could be thoughts that trigger feelings of resentment in you, such as, he wasn't there for this or that, and I was left to fend for myself.

114. It could be: he was busy. I was drowning.

115. It could also be: I was trying to help. That was silly of me.

116. Or that he never took exercise.

117. He didn't make an effort for me.
118. He didn't want me.
119. Try not to resist, avoid or turn away. Simply let the thoughts and feelings come to the surface while you are working. See yourself bent over on a cushion in the garden with a sponge in your hand. See that you are busy, absorbed in what you are doing by the light of the torch, and that your thoughts and feelings are bobbing to the surface now and then.
   Notice them for what they are.
120. Don't judge!

No question the chest would have to be axed open and butterflied. She would be some time at the barbecue. That was fine. There was enough fuel, and she'd had some wine: she would stand through the night with a bonfire blazing with what was left of the furniture. She tapped the head torch to bring the bulb back to life, and then crouched down beside the torso, using her fingers this time to test the skin. She moved her hands all over it, squatting down to get them around the ribs.

His heart was still in there; that would have to be cut out, and eaten separately, if she could manage it, in a recipe of its own.

She rocked the torso about on the plastic and saw how bits of soil and turf from the dug-up lawn leaped on. The dog was barking in the kitchen, and Lizzie switched her head torch off and sat very still in the garden for a moment while the sound died down.

The agent would say: "We're not entirely sure why they decided to dig up the garden. Something to do with wanting to plant a meadow, we think."

$$\uparrow\!\!\uparrow$$

121. Try to understand that your mind will offer up all sorts of excuses and diversions.

122. Burying bits of him in the garden, or out in the woods, even that thought of a sky burial, are just the sorts of diversions I'm referring to.

123. Let the ideas come, but stay resolute. Disposing of a body in this way has already passed your own various tests. It's practical, economical, and in many ways a moral choice. See below.

124. It doesn't matter, either, if you haven't given thought to any test whatsoever. Don't be sitting there thinking, what test? I never ran it past anything in me.

125. Remember, some people think and worry about things more than others. If you're the sort of person who wouldn't have any kind of test, that doesn't matter in the least.

126. One could argue that disposing of him in a lake would be good for the water life. Similarly, burying

a body in the garden would fertilize the soil and add all sorts of welcome nutrients to the feeders in there. But eating him is nourishing a human who was, let's face it, undernourished. And not just physically so. The process will be strengthening the psyche and readying you for your journey onward in life.

127. On that last point, do not think, if you are a little overweight, or heavier than you'd like to be, "Oh, I am fat, and therefore shouldn't be doing this." It doesn't matter what size you are. You can still eat your husband.

128. Also worth bearing in mind that while a burial might be good for the ground or water, it would cause merry hell out in the world if found. Which, of course, it is much more likely to be.

129. In the first instance, you wouldn't want anyone else to come across a bit of him unawares. Imagine a child walking in the woods and finding his hand!

130. Thank goodness, then, that his hand has been absorbed into you, and not left out in the woods to traumatize an innocent child.

131. Consider also the people who will be spared images of body parts found in the garden or woods. This includes those working for the police, forensic experts and random people, in the Dog and Duck, for example, who might see the images on the television and then not sleep for a week.

132. Obviously, it's not likely that a random person having a drink in the Dog and Duck and seeing a human hand on the television is going to lose sleep for a whole week, even one night, but it might be something to consider as you go along.

133. Mike and Nic? Young love, and full of cake. Your cake! Consider them. How would they feel?

134. Do all that you can to divert your attention from thoughts of giving up.

135. Resist any vague, absentminded impulse to check in the mirror for facial hair or brawn. Absorbing a man doesn't make you...Just as eating beef or pork...

9

That night, while the bust of her husband was defrosting in the garden, Lizzie sat at the kitchen table in her nightie. She had her coat around her shoulders and a glass of white wine in her hand. She opened up the laptop.

> *Hi, Joanna. This is Lizzie Prain. I'm using his email account to let you know that Jacob has left me and gone to live abroad.*
>
> *He met someone. She was an escort girl from a place in Guildford called the Pearl. They have eloped.*
>
> *He won't be coming back and I am closing his account down now. Goodbye.*

She signed her name. Then she went back and deleted it. She pressed send. She went to his sent items and read the email through. An email came back with a ping. Under the table Lizzie tucked her foot under the dog's stomach.

> *Hi! Good to hear from you!*
> *I hope you're all right. Thank you for letting me*

know. If I can do anything, or help in any way, I'd like
you to be in touch. OK?
    All best wishes,
    Joanna

Lizzie read the email through. It had come back un-
believably quickly. She tried to run a hand through her
hair. She looked around the little kitchen and lit a cigarette.

Thank you, she wrote. And sent.

A reply bounced back at once: *No problem.*

Lizzie felt her heart skip a little. She wrote: *I hope you*
don't mind.

> *Mind what?*
> *That I have written at this time of night.*

Lizzie sat and massaged her jaw.

> *Not at all. I'm doing a degree. Always do my study-*
> *ing in the middle of the night. I don't get very much*
> *done, as it happens. I spend far too much time on the*
> *Internet reading articles that have nothing to do with*
> *my course. Are you all right?*

Lizzie began to chew on a fingernail. She didn't re-
spond. Joanna sent another email.

Course you are. Sorry.

Sorry for what?

For asking. For prying. I'm too damn nosy for my own good. Do you want to go on to Chat?

Lizzie wrote: *No.* She didn't know what Chat was. She wrote: *Goodbye.* Then she put *sorry* and deleted it because it made her sound foolish. She didn't even know what she was sorry for. She hadn't wanted a conversation with this woman in the first place. "Wasn't I perfectly all right without?" she said aloud, and she shut the computer down.

By now Rita was lying at the top of the stairs with her belly sticking out like a football. As Lizzie came up the stairs Rita opened an eye and made a low whining sound.

"I know, Rita," Lizzie whispered, as she stepped over her and went on into the bathroom.

🍴

136. No comment!

137. Actually, yes comment: of course you were all right. What on earth made you think you might like to talk to this woman, beyond letting her know that Jacob had gone and left you?

138. No feeling for companionship or intimacy at this

crucial stage in your preparation for departure can be considered rational.

139. You are not having a normal human experience. Defrosting your husband's upper body in the garden in preparation for roast and consumption is not "everyday"! Go to Guildford and shop if you have to. Buy a bra. Do anything. But do not try to make friends right now!

140. Resist!

By two the following afternoon the barbecue was once again lit.

Lizzie was sitting some way off from it on the end of a garden chair. The axe was at her feet.

She was drinking black tea, and smoking a cigarette, the ash of which she simply flicked into the grass. Her red lipstick was smeared now. The dog was lying at her feet, stomach still distended.

There was a bad smell all around them, and the day was gray and bleak.

In the kitchen, the lettuce was washed; it was in the colander, crisp, white and clean. Lizzie had cut two tomatoes into quarters. The rest of the cucumber had been sliced. She'd run out of dressing, but that didn't matter. She was much too full of fat.

In the garden she put the axe in the air and brought it down right in the middle of his chest. It made only a dent. Gripping the handle, she knelt down on the grass; she looked at the sky.

Her mother had said: "You're tall. You're not going to fit in anywhere. Making art forces you to be different. You have to be. You can't be the same as anyone else."

She didn't have talent for drawing. She hadn't wanted to express herself. She'd found a job instead. And a house. He'd asked her to move in. She'd asked him if she could move in.

She had liked taking care of him.

They had walked in the woods, side by side.

Like a little girl taking care of a doll. On the lawn she looked in and up, and cut out the heart with the fruit knife.

Then the lungs came out. They were dark, purple jelly: two slippery pale sacs. She held them in her hands and then laid them on the grass before they were bagged and labeled and put in the freezer.

Split in two, his chest was still huge, like wings, and red with blood. She lifted his left side onto the barbecue.

She put her hands in her pockets and walked away as the barbecue caught and flamed. She smelled it. She turned around and looked at her feet and she looked at the gray light on the garden, and over the wall towards the trees, but there wasn't anything to see or feel.

Marriage had been marriage—nothing more or less than what it had been—but the persistent feeling in Lizzie Prain had something to do with time wasted, seeing them both through their various depressions with food and the preservation of everyday life according to the body's needs. Very little had been got for it. So, going to prison for manslaughter felt like more waste, she thought, tipping a bottle of rib sauce onto the side sitting on the barbecue. She watched the flames leap up and catch, and the air filled with the smoke. She feared the people in the prison as much as she feared the hours in a cell. She knew there were activities and projects for prisoners—initiatives launched by well-meaning citizens on the outside—but the idea that someone in prison would be able to use their pragmatism to any effect seemed too far-fetched. Lizzie lifted the ribs with tongs and an oven glove and carried them over to the picnic spot she had laid out on the cold grass.

10

She ate what she could that night and then went through the house to the porch. She stood for an hour in the porch but Mike didn't come with the money for the cake. She kept thinking she heard the sound of his wheels in the lane, but it was only the wind in the trees and the cars up on the hill.

In the kitchen she put the light on and opened up the laptop. She had a tea towel wrapped around her neck, and the towel was covered in sauce. On the table was a cup of Earl Grey tea with milk.

Are you there, Joanna?

On the piece of paper beside her she wrote:

My name is Lizzie Prain. In a week or two I will be done here. And then I will be on a train to Scotland. I will find a room. I will find somewhere, a room somewhere, a bed to lay my head. It will be clean.

Yes, I'm here.

Lizzie breathed.

Oh good, she wrote. *Thank God.*

She deleted "God" and put "you" instead. She wrote *Thank you* twice more. And then deleted that too. How silly that writing words down and sending them out to someone made her feel so foolish.

> *Are you all right, Lizzie?*
> *Yes. I am. It's just that I'm trying to get away from here and start over again. It's not as easy as I'd thought it would be. That's all. There seems such an awful lot to get through.*

There was a pause.

> *Is there anything I can do to help you?*
> *Can I ask you something?*
> *Course!*
> *How was he?*

Lizzie waited. She took a sip of tea.

> *When you saw him last?*
> *Not himself. I did know that times were hard. By that I mean I know that things had become tricky financially. He didn't want to stay in the afternoon and talk, as he had usually done. We had a very quick sandwich. He asked if I liked the sculpture. I didn't. He said*

that was fine, and just wrapped it back up in newspaper and made for the door. Then he turned and said he was thinking of going away. He said he hadn't spoken to you about it because he imagined you wouldn't care one way or the other. He seemed, I don't know.

There was a pause. Lizzie waited, staring at the screen.

It was as if he'd been working on something and then just driven up in the car with the plaster and dust all over him still. I thought that if someone was going away to start again then shouldn't there be some sort of vitality in that? Shouldn't there be a spark?

He was right, wrote Lizzie. *I don't care. I don't give a damn!!*

That's OK!
What is?
How long's it been?
What?
Since he went away?
Some time now.
Do you know that I saw him again, after that time at Christmas? He came up on Boxing Day. I'd said on email that we were busy with family but he said he was coming up anyway, that you had people to

see, or something to do. So he was going to be in the area, and he asked if he could pop in. I said we were tied up.

He came anyway, I know, Lizzie wrote. She took a sip of tea. She still had the cloth with the sauce around her neck.

Around four in the afternoon. He rang the bell. We had people for lunch. It was still going on. He just came on in and joined us.

He told me you'd invited him to lunch, Joanna. He went up first thing in the morning.

We hadn't. But it didn't really matter.

Another pause.

Really sorry, by the way.

For what?

That I never thanked you for that lovely lunch. It was so nice to sit in your garden. And the food was really delicious. But I should have returned the invitation and asked you to come here.

It's all right.

It's not really.

Well, it doesn't matter now!

Last Easter, when he came up with the sculpture of the bucket and spade, he said things were really aw-

ful. That you'd started the cakes business together and that it was losing money. He said that if he were ever to leave and try and go somewhere to start again, then I could come to the house and just help myself to what was left in his studio.

His what?

His studio.

Lizzie smiled. She turned to the window and stared at the dark.

Do you remember a studio from when you came here?

No. I remember the shed, and the garage had some bits and pieces in. He said you'd had a studio built.

Not here.

No?

No.

A pause.

He must have meant that I could come and take a look at the shed. Do you think that might be all right? I've been thinking about it quite a lot since you got in touch with me, Lizzie. I wondered if I might come down this weekend if that's convenient?

No. Not this weekend. I'm really busy. I doubt I can manage it before I go away. But if there is anything of his, I will make sure it gets to you. His stuff is of no interest to me since I think it's all…

Lizzie flicked a tear from the corner of her eye and ripped the tea towel off her neck.

Are you there, Lizzie?
I have to go now, Joanna. I am sorry. Goodbye.

🍴

141. Consider putting the laptop in the back of the Volvo now and driving it first thing in the morning to the municipal dump off the A31. You could be free of it!
142. There will be a man there in an orange boilersuit who will gladly take it from you.
143. Wipe all emails. Shut down accounts.
144. Wipe all Word documents.
145. Pour yourself a brandy and get some sleep.

In the morning, she rang the gas board. The woman said she could do what she liked with the gas and electricity supply to her own home. She didn't have to sound so apologetic. Yes, of course she could settle her bill now if she wanted to, or leave it till she was ready to go.

The same happened with the water. The water man

was nice. And the woman at the council was on her last day before leaving to have a baby. No probs, she said. No probs at all.

"I'll be gone by the end of the month," said Lizzie. "I can't say for sure when the new people will be moving in."

Monday was bright. It felt like starting again. Lizzie put red lipstick on in the bathroom and drove like the wind to the Wild Oaks garden center. Jacob's heart was in a glass bowl of water, in the fridge.

She saw Tom as soon as she arrived. He was standing outside the entrance moving bags of compost. Tom had been eight, his sisters ten, when she'd done the babysitting for them up at the farm. She had tried to be a proper neighbor and had made herself useful—tidying, washing, doing the laundry; more useful, perhaps, than she'd needed to be. She'd made a real effort with Barbara, using all sorts of helpful hand gestures to illustrate the words coming from her mouth. She hadn't realized that Barbara was only partially deaf, and they hadn't thought to stop her and explain this.

"You've been nice, Liz," Erik had said, blocking her exit. "Ever so nice," he'd said, and then he'd asked her to join them for a meal.

She'd run back down the lane in the dark on her long legs, clutching her cake tin.

A few days later Tom had appeared—a beautiful,

dark-haired little boy—and asked if there were any more cakes. She'd bent down on the steps outside and given him some bread and jam that he'd devoured while she'd walked him back up the lane.

There had been one occasion when the family had come to the bend in the lane with three teenagers for a barbecue. The wasps had clung to the ketchup bottle. Jacob had come in and out of the house all day with that long look on his face. And Lizzie had darted in and out of the kitchen behind him, unable to say anything at all.

It had only happened once. She'd slapped him the night before. She hadn't meant to hurt him. Of course she hadn't. It had come out of nowhere, a reaction to something long gone, she'd thought. Something he'd said about her not needing more, not having the imagination to know what more there was in life. What more there was of what? she'd asked him, though he'd chosen not to reply.

Had he meant of love? Had he meant there was more love out there, like the love that came from a person like Joanna? Had Joanna become, in his imagination, a richer source of love?

Years later, when Lizzie had come to the garden center for the barbecue, she'd told the nice young man how she was getting on with her cake business.

He'd bent down and reached underneath the barbecue, showing her what to do with the gas pipe. She'd seen the skin on his back.

Days like that with the wasps and the faces and the light in the woods stuck out like a broken bone when you looked back, and Tom would have known that something was wrong with the marriage between the two people in the lane.

Now she sat in her car and watched him across the car park. His shoulders were big and round like knuckles, his arms dangling.

The best thing about not having too much imagination, Lizzie's mother had said to her when she was a girl, was not having to take the extra disappointments. It had never been clear, then, whether she felt her daughter did have imagination. Lizzie had brought the issue into the marriage with her. She'd talked about it with Jacob. He'd not said that it was absurd, and wrong, and plain rude and "Who in their right mind could dream of saying that to another person? Who would have the gumption?" He'd shrugged instead. And when he started wandering off, Lizzie had the feeling that he was going off to imagine things, to be away from her so that his own wild figuring wasn't stunted, or stifled, or crushed, by the great absence of hers.

It was weird. The way people behaved.

What people did to each other.

She reached into the back of her bag for her lipstick and reapplied.

Then she got out of the car and walked towards the entrance.

Tom Vickory saw her coming, and shook a hand in the air, smiling. Her heart thumped.

"Hi," he said, and he held out his hand. There was a flash of plaster on his finger.

"Blimey," he said, and looked away. He jiggled his shoulders as if trying to shake something off them. He bent over, then straightened up and back, and took such a huge breath it looked like he was drowning. Lizzie looked back into the empty car park.

"Stuff will come up," he said, as if he was reading out of a book. "When you least expect it."

"Is there something wrong?" she asked him.

"No," said Tom. He smiled. "How are you?"

"I'm fine," said Lizzie, frowning.

"Are you here for something in particular?" he asked her.

"I've come for barbecue tongs and rubber gloves. And firelighters, and a gas cylinder." She also needed bin liners, dishcloths, steel to sharpen a knife.

Lizzie followed Tom through the shop, her eye on the desert boots he was wearing. He stopped in front of the drills.

"How is your sister?" Lizzie said. "How is Nic?"

"We think she might have freaked out a bit. She's sort of gone. We don't know where. She's got her phone, but we can't get hold of her. Mike took her to see a mate of hers. She took off from there, without the friend."

Tom seemed to be in some sort of pain. He grimaced

and put a hand up to his chest, and fiddled with a small white button on his Aertex.

"Man!" he said, and he made a little burping sound as if trying to release something from his throat. "Powerful energy," he said.

"I beg your pardon?"

"Just energy, man."

"Is it coming from me?"

"Nah," he said, and he smiled, and put a hand on her shoulder, which made Lizzie jump.

"It probably is," she said, feeling hot. She remembered the red lipstick she was wearing. It was an effort towards strengthening her resolve, towards self-love: it was a way of saying to the world, "I know what I am doing."

146. If a girl from the farm has disappeared for reasons that cannot be explained, it may lead to a little local disruption that you do not need to be involved in. Or close to.

147. Don't speak to anyone. Close down the email account.

148. Don't talk to Joanna.

149. Don't talk to Tom.

150. His heart is in the fridge. Set to on that.

151. Just before the onset of a depression, there will be what feels like an obsessive experience of desire. You will want to be taken in arms. This is fine. You are in mad, desperate flight from yourself.
152. Gaze longingly at young men if you want to. It's entirely normal. Stare at wrists and thighs and the muscles in their necks at the petrol station with your car window down.

Lizzie put the key in the ignition and drove out of the garden center car park. She glanced across at the boy's cheek and inhaled the scent of him. He was sitting beside her in a navy Puffa coat and jogging bottoms. As she drove onto the dual carriageway, she lifted her head to check her face in the mirror.

She stopped in a lay-by, got out of the car, and stood in the air with her head up. Across the top of the field there was a band of very bright yellow light. There was a fluttering sensation in her stomach. She waited to be sick.

She hadn't slept. The house was almost clear now, everything burned; the bloody bits of the lawn dug up. The bag was packed by the bedroom door. She was almost done. She was nearly there. She stared at the light across the top of the field and felt her head moving towards it. In the freezer, still to be eaten, were the arms, the head and another thigh. The dark little house in the lane would be closed down soon, left behind, a memory.

There would be a seat in a train carriage. It would pull north. The day would be bright. It would all be future, and open, and clean, and light. It would be possible to do this, to break away.

In the passenger seat Tom Vickory was staring forward through the windscreen. Lizzie got back in. He put a hand to his chest again and grimaced.

Lizzie didn't make a sound. She was much too shy to talk to the boy while he was sitting beside her in the car rubbing his palms up and down his trouser legs. She waited for him to stop doing that, and for some words to come into her mind.

She slowed down as she came to the village, and went past the steamed-up mirror on the bend. She drove past the Dog and Duck. She turned into Tubford Lane and glanced over at him.

"Would it be all right if I come in?" he asked. "There's no one at home till later and I haven't got my key."

"I'm afraid not," said Lizzie.

"Come again?"

"No."

He laughed. He looked over at her as they bumped up the lane.

"What do you mean?"

"Why did you leave work?"

"I'm not feeling great."

"What is it?"

"I'm run-down. I think it's that."

Lizzie said that he couldn't come in.

"I'll sit in the garden."

"No. That doesn't work either," she said, and her cheeks were a deep, flaming red.

It wouldn't work because she was now so determined to be done with the grim business at home that all she could think of was taking another piece out of the freezer and getting on with it. Then the house would be locked. She would be at Euston in two hours. She'd take the dog.

She parked the car in the lane and looked at the clock on the dashboard, at the speedometer, and the petrol gauge. She had no idea what information she was looking for. It would be cool inside the train. There would be a seat for her, a place for Rita, a cup of coffee to buy. There was always, in every place on earth, a cup of coffee to buy. The train would draw out of the station, and pull north. It would carry them all the way.

Tom didn't move. He sat back in his seat, staring forward.

"My grandfather thinks your husband left last Monday. He said he saw him out with the dog on the Sunday."

Lizzie turned to his face and then looked beyond it to the wing mirror on his side. Jacob had taken the dog out for a walk on the Sunday night. He'd been thinking about going for a run.

"He did leave, last Monday," she said.

"But how does my grandfather know that?"

Lizzie shrugged. Her lips were pressed together.

"He said he then saw you on the common. More recently. He said he was shouting at you. Then he said your husband wasn't here anymore. Not 'here,' he said," and Tom held four fingers up like dicky birds either side of his sarcastic smile and his brown sorrowful eyes.

11

Tom Vickory came into the house and went with her through the hall and into the living room. He moved the air around and changed the atmosphere. Lizzie sniffed the air behind him as he walked past her to look around. She took the Pearl receipt from underneath the bowl on the windowsill and showed it to him. Tom took it from her and gave it back, said she had nothing to prove.

She sniffed the air in the doorway to the living room and then went to make a fire while he took his coat off and sat down on the sofa, splaying his knees apart. He fiddled with his phone. She had left a window open.

Tom put the phone back in his bag and inched forward, stretching his arms down and spreading his hands on the floor. He lifted his head. He said it was cool how there was nothing in the house. "I feel like I can breathe," he said.

Lizzie lit the fire and blew into it so that the smell of ashes from the night before would drift around the room a little.

"Mike said you'd mentioned to him about renting the house."

She lingered around the fireplace. He was watching her, smiling shyly.

"Just an idea," she said. "He asked me to make a cake. I asked if he was interested, for him and your sister."

"Have to be cheap," said Tom. "They ain't got much cash." Then he shrugged and looked like he didn't want to continue that conversation.

"Where's your dog?"

"She runs off sometimes. Not to worry, though. She comes back." Her voice trailed off. She stood by the fireplace with her legs straight and her arms straight. She was in her jeans and coat.

"Can't believe I just bunked off for the day."

"Is that what you did?"

"Basically," he said. She looked at his feet.

"Will they take you back?"

"Yeah, course. I'm the best they've got. Tomorrow'll be fine. Someone'll cover for me today."

"Would you like a tea or coffee, Tom?"

"Tea would be great."

"I have a herbal tea."

"Lovely!"

He put a hand to his chest again and took in a huge breath.

"What are you doing?"

"Feeling."

Lizzie's eyes dilated with fear.

Tom said: "Nic'll be back. She's done this before. I'm

not surprised. Just freaks out. Like the dog. The girls can't stand Mum and Dad. Mum and Dad can't stand the girls. But they're all kind of hooked on it, if you know what I mean. All bound up. If we're having baked potatoes, Mum grates the cheese on, Dad has extra. The girls pick it off. No one says anything, but it's all in-wardly fucked. The farm's fucked. I'd go tomorrow too, if I could. I think I will. You know? I think I could just go right now."

Lizzie said nothing. She watched his limbs being thrown around on the sofa as he made himself more comfortable. She smiled and moved past him with her hands folded in front of her, and she went into the kitchen and sniffed. She made a pot of tea. They would drink this, she thought, and then he would go.

Tom called through to ask if she needed any help.

"No, I'm fine," she said, and she could hear the brightness in her voice. Very quickly she mixed up a cake and threw it in the oven.

She came back into the living room with a pot of pep-permint tea. "I thought you might like a bit of sponge," she said.

"You made a cake?" he said, yawning, when she came back in. He was like a great, stretching cat.

Lizzie sat on the floor beside the fireplace.

"It'll be just a little while," she said. "It's in the oven now."

"Wow," he said. "Great!" He had a very big goofy smile.

"I suppose you think that makes me frumpy."

Tom laughed.

"Not at all!" he said, lifting his sweatshirt and rubbing his hard brown stomach. "I'm bloody starving, to be honest!"

$$\text{\Large ᵞᵞ}$$

153. You. Have. The. Remains. Of. Your. Dead. Husband. In. The. Freezer.

154. You. Were. The. Murderer.

155. The. Freezer. Is. In. The. Garage. Through. The. Interconnecting. Door. To. Your. Kitchen.

156. The. Heart. Is. In. The. Fridge!

157. Suggest. You. Get. The. Young. Man. In. The. Green. Aertex. Out. Of. Your. Living. Room.

Lizzie knelt in front of the fire, the teapot on the floor, and placed her hands flat on her thighs. She couldn't look him in the eye. It made her feel intensely itchy and uncomfortable.

"You OK?" he said.

She made a very calm face by emptying everything out of it.

"Yes, I'm fine."

"Really?"

"Yes!"

"How do you feel? Right now," he said, and she knew that he was smiling because she felt that as a presence in the room, and it was warm and comforting, and so her head leaned further to the right and the smile on her face seemed to grow ever wider and more crazed with the awkward thrilling realization of desire.

On the sofa, Tom pressed the cake into his mouth. He dropped crumbs all over the place, but didn't apologize. He looked at his feet, occasionally took one of his huge breaths, lifting his neck right up, but he didn't say anything about the house or about the husband. She was grateful for that. She sat and beamed.

They ate the cake and drank some tea. He didn't say thank you.

He said, "I think I'll stretch out and have some zizz. That all right?"

She nodded. She wasn't thinking. She felt gracious and kind. Poor boy. He was tired.

When she got up, she could feel his eyes on the back of her. She smoothed her jumper down and smiled at him, but his eyes were hidden in the crook of his arm.

158. The closer you get to the innards, the more resistance you will feel. Your mind does not want your body to ingest the intimate parts of another human being. This has long been struck off the record of human experience.

159. All kinds of strange scenarios will appear to you, which are events you yourself will have created in order to forestall the project.

160. This is called SELF-SABOTAGE!

161. Do not be surprised if you find yourself fantasizing about kissing a stranger, or running into the road to end up in the accident and emergency ward of your local hospital.

162. You may well be picking at an old emotional wound. This is diversion.

163. If you do find yourself with a man in your house, you will know you have made a serious error of judgment. Remove him.

164. Go outside in your coat and take a walk.

165. Braise the heart.

166. It will be high in protein, iron, calcium and magnesium.

167. It has worked hard for fifty-five years. It will be lean. Like all muscle it will become tough if cooked too quickly.

168. Serve it with something clean and bitter. An endive or celery salad, dill, fennel; any of the above will go nicely.

*   *   *

The heart was larger than she'd expected, slightly bigger than her fist. It was like holding a root ball. She washed it carefully in her hands, then placed it on the chopping board and took her sharpest knife. It was manageable though; and she could fit her hands around it. Unlike the two great pieces of chest, which had flamed like ships on the barbecue the night before last and brought her to tears. She removed the tendons, tubes and tougher flaps of skin around the edge. These she would give to the dog. She turned the oven up to 150 degrees, and put some water on to boil through a percolator for coffee. From the vegetable box in the garage she took two onions and a parsnip. She brought these inside with an old carrot, some garlic, and three potatoes. She cubed the potatoes, and arranged them in a glass baking dish. She mixed the vegetables with her hands, and then placed the heart on top and poured on three cups of broth. She sprinkled half a teaspoon of salt and half a teaspoon of pepper in an even layer. Then she covered the dish with foil and slid it into the oven. It would need to be cooked for three hours before she checked it, stirred the ingredients and added more beef broth if needed. It would then go back in for another two hours. It would be ready to eat by the middle of the afternoon.

She sat at the kitchen table with a cup of coffee, and leaned her head back against the wall.

For a long time she felt the color draining from her cheeks. She watched the clock.

Tom was still here. He came into the kitchen coughing and said, "Right, that's it, I'm going to change."

Lizzie was sitting very still on the kitchen chair. She had decided today was the day for cooking the heart and nothing was going to deter her. The boy wasn't here to notice her cooking. He was hanging around, in limbo, waiting for life to make use of him. He hadn't looked at the oven.

He sat down across from her and faced out towards the window. He took his mobile out of his back pocket and put it on the table. Lizzie felt the sweat under her arms. She stared at the oven. She wanted him to leave. Tom was sitting on the front of his chair, looking very alert, with his hands resting on his knees. He closed his eyes, and breathed in through his nose. It was possible that he was preparing to meditate. Lizzie started to shake. She looked at the shiny dark hair, and his perfect, smooth skin.

He carried on sitting there, breathing. After a while he opened his eyes. He coughed again. He twisted the button through the buttonhole on his Aertex. He did not seem to notice the woman sitting opposite him, white and shaking. Or if he did, he was too polite to say a word.

"Nic's problem's anxiety," he said. "Always has been.

Being young. Comparatively speaking. Like to her mates. Mike's a nice guy, though. He loves her. He's solid. Reliable sort. It's what she needs. Certain she loves him." He paused, opened his eyes and twisted his phone around on the table.

"Fuck, I need to move out, man!"

He looked at her now and two tears squeezed out of his eyes.

"You could live here," said Lizzie. Then she turned to look out of the window.

The wind was blowing in the tops of the trees.

From the corner of her eye she saw him turn his head very quickly, almost as if he'd been anticipating the comment. She flicked her eyes at him and saw that he was frowning. It didn't put her off. It had become a plan. She would offer this. Then he would go.

"You could live here with Mike and Nic. If you wanted to. I was thinking of converting the shed. I need the rent, and...It's big enough. If we cleared it out, we could make it a perfectly adequate space."

She thought of it, of the young man living inside the shed. She thought about him being here with her. That would be perfect, she felt. To be alone here, with him in the garden.

Tom made a little snorting sound while dragging a finger across his eye.

"Yeah, right, I can live *here*."

"It's cheap," said Lizzie.

"Think what Mum and Dad would say," he said. "If we all decamped down here!" He grinned again, hands still flat on his knees, back straight.

"There's a carpet. And some lamps in there. We could get you a heater, and some curtains. Mike and Nic could do the house, couldn't they? You'd just have the shed to sort. And you're practical. You could get everything from work."

He laughed. She looked. His back was very long. He hadn't noticed the smell in the kitchen, hadn't asked what was cooking in the oven. It was a rich, dark, disgusting smell. It was her husband's dark little heart.

"The garden's got potential," he said.

He twisted round to look at her.

"How much?" he said.

"You could have the shed for free. It's big enough to live in. And you could make the garden your own."

Tom put a hand under his T-shirt and rubbed his stomach till a small, polite burp came up. He was restless and larky, trying to show he didn't care one way or another, but Lizzie could see that something else was going on, something under the surface was turning, lifting a forlorn little face towards her smile.

In the lane he kissed her cheek. He squeezed her shoulder and said, "Thank you." It sounded as if it was coming from the bottom of his heart. She squinted in the sunlight.

"Thanks for the lift and the cake," he said.

"No problem!"

"You're feeling scared," he said. "Aren't you?"

Lizzie stepped back. He was leaving, and grinning, and telling her what she felt, with his gums exposed. She saw that his ears were an odd sort of shape; that the lobes were barely there, and the ear just slid inwards straight to his head. She tried to recall Jacob's lobes.

"Can I come again?" he said.

Lizzie looked down at her feet. She smiled and tilted her head to one side because she didn't know how to reply. Then she turned and went inside to boil water for the spaghetti. She could soften a shallot and some garlic in a little butter and chop the cooked beefy heart in to flash-fry in the pan. With a few forkfuls of spaghetti, she thought, it would go down fine.

🍴

169. Right. He's gone. Good.
170. Make a timetable and stick it up on the wall.
171. Write down what is left to get through and start thinking about the order in which you're going to do it.
172. If you've now given yourself a deadline, you will have to do a bit of work on yourself in order to speed the process and ensure completion.

173. Start thinking of your stomach as a pit. Try to imagine, sitting with both feet flat on the floor on a kitchen chair, that the pit is being opened, as if by a machine in a quarry.

Lynn from the hotel made a call to her mobile.

Driving with the phone on the front seat of the car, Lizzie saw the screen light up blue. She put her indicator on, and pulled onto the verge. She was near the lake, and water dripped from the trees onto the windscreen of the Volvo.

"We like you," said Lynn. "We think you'll be a perfect fit."

Lizzie sat very still, like a mouse, her nose twitching in the hood of her raincoat. Her feet were on the pedals still, resting there in Wellingtons, ready to drive on.

"We'd like to offer you the job. Starting as soon as we can get the paperwork done. Give us a few weeks. We're thinking of a little bonus structure to add to the equation. You get lunch here, and use of all the facilities, of course. Pool, sauna, Jacuzzi, health club, car park."

There was a breath. Lizzie clung to the phone.

"Steven is saying well done, Liz!"

Lizzie felt anxiety ripple through her stomach, and a tingling in her hands. They all called her Liz now. Even Tom Vickory had said it.

"Bye, Liz. See you."

Lizzie sat back in the driver's seat.

More drops of rain plopped onto the windscreen. In the garden the soil was mulched and wet and rich with worms from rain in the night. The garden was churned up; and the house was clean. In the back of the car, the dog barked. For a moment she had it all. She had her health, and she had a home with a garden. She had a car she could get about in, a correspondent, a neighbor. And she had something to do. She clutched hold of the phone still and pressed it into her ear.

🍴

174. If, when driving, or walking, you need to stop to be sick, simply try to accept that this is happening and try not to fight it. Slow the car down, pull over, open the door, and get out. Leaning out, in the hope that you will be able to do it in this position cleanly, is hopeless. If you have the time, take the key from the ignition, shut the door behind you, and bend right over. Be sick properly.

175. Get some mints, some tissues, and a bottle of water from the petrol station, and keep these items in the car at all times.

176. Take the car through a car wash. Stay in the car for the duration of the wash. When the horizontal pole dispensing a torrent of water and soapsuds

comes slowly towards you inciting terror and an urge to cry, simply go with it.

177. While the wash is on and you are inside the storm, feel free to bawl and scream and howl.

178. Obviously, you're not going to be able to take the job!

"It's all mine," he'd said about the house and garden. His face had crinkled as he smiled. He'd taken a cigarette out from behind his ear.

Upstairs, the bed for her had been made up with soft blankets. It was a small, narrow room, and dark. It had a window overlooking the back of the house with its huge, unkempt garden which gave way, eventually, to trees. She'd stood at the window, looking out into the wet, dark woods. He'd called her down, offered her whiskey for her throat.

"Think breasts," he'd said, and got some paper out to show her what the lane was like. "Two breasts, and both are covered in sandy soil. Conifer on one," to which he added diagonal lines, "and then a mixture," scribbled, "of oak and broadleaf on the other.

"We're in the middle, in the cleavage," he'd said, pointing to hers. "It's dark and damp and the woods down here are mostly alder." Then he'd drawn two wiggly roughly parallel lines from the cleavage up to the head, which was where the farm was.

"I don't really know them," he'd said. "But they might

be looking for someone to help out. And I was thinking maybe I'd get a dog at some point."

There was an opportunity here then. They might be looking for someone up at the farm. The man in the house on the bend might get a puppy. Maybe she'd warm up, Lizzie had thought. Maybe she'd be safe. Maybe here she'd become less numb.

Tom

She'd left the key for me under the mat. There was a note on the kitchen table with instructions. Nic hadn't come back and things were grim and snappy up at the farm. I was glad to be out of there. I told them I'd do what I could to help if I was needed, and that they could get hold of me at the house on the bend. My grandfather had a chest infection. He'd been up all night coughing in the kitchen. Something wrong with that place, he said. He was dying. Something wrong with ours too, I replied.

I was excited, nervous, determined; I felt like a kid who'd come across a hideout and was going to make it his camp. I felt like the world could just go on and I was going to be all right because I had this thing to think about, to fully occupy my mind. I went in. It was cold in there. I put the lights on. Lizzie had kept the electricity running. I switched them off again to save it. Rita was sitting on her bed in the kitchen, waiting for me to come.

Lizzie had burned or dumped almost everything else in the house—out of revenge, I think—and I loved that sense of emptiness and space. It was like walking into a brand-new studio and crouching down to plan a life. I looked around to see if she'd left anything for me. There was a vase of tulips on the table, and a note. Otherwise, there was nothing. I jumped up and down. I threw my arms in the air. I went into the garden and shouted at the trees.

Dear Tom,

I don't know how long I'll be, but here is my mobile number in case you need anything.

There's been nothing back from Mike and Nic about renting the house because of her going off, but it probably wasn't going to work anyway and it doesn't matter to me just at the moment. I'll find someone in due course.

Rita's food is in one of the green bins in the garage. If you could take her out for a walk in the morning and in the evening that would be great.

Do what you feel like doing in the garden. I'll leave it to you.

The shed could do with clearing still, just a few things left that I didn't have time to take away. You'll find three small figurines in there. These are my husband's sculptures. I'm going to try and organize for a woman who liked his pieces to come and get them. Perhaps just keep them on the kitchen table for the moment.

The freezer in the garage is being collected on Wednesday. It seems huge, but it'll fit through the big metal door. The button for that is on the right wall, as you go in from the kitchen. You'll see the number for the freezer men. Feel free to call them if there are any problems.

"Let go," I said to myself. It sounds easy. But try living in my head. Same old shit as everyone else. Same old clichés. And sooner or later we have to let go of the stories, because they make everything worse. It doesn't matter, all that shit. Stay with what's here, what is. All that green, and the feel of my naked feet on the tarmac, the muscles in my legs, and the smell of trees.

I wanted to be away from all that crap we tell ourselves. Up at the farm they were all quietly rotting, being pulled down by something no one could explain. "Let go," I said, over and over.

It was my day off. I moved around her house, opening drawers and shutting things. There wasn't much there— she'd left kitchen utensils, knives, tin opener, saucepans, a single vase, an apron out drying on the line.

I spent most of the first day in the garden. I raked over the ashes from the bonfire, and spread them out through the grass. In the week I'd be laying down new turf and putting compost under the azaleas and the rhododendron. Lizzie had said to spend a little money on some new tools for the garden, so I put some hooks on the back of the shed door in preparation for the rake, and the spade and trimmer and a nice new broom that I'd get for her. The shed was mostly clear. I took the last bits out and filled a couple of bin liners, and I found the figures and put them on the table as she'd asked me to do, and then I gave the shed floor a good sweep. I didn't really think it would make a proper room, but I hadn't seen it yet with a bed, a lamp and chair. For the moment I slept upstairs in her room. She'd left a mattress, and a sheet, a duvet, two pillows.

12

In the sink were the liver, spleen, kidneys and lungs, fully defrosted and ready to go into sausages. Some she would have for breakfast. The rest would go in the cassoulet with fat from the buttocks defrosting now on the garage floor.

His crown jewels were going in the cassoulet too. Boiled, then chopped.

She felt the sneer on her face; there was a muscle by her left nostril that seemed permanently stiffened, as if it had been on recoil now for thirteen days.

She put the liver, spleen, kidneys and lungs in a glass dish organizer she had used for crisps and dips.

The spleen was dark and bloody, and small. In her mind, his organs had been larger than this, lurking around inside him like dark fish. But here they all were: little ordinary lumps spinning round in the microwave.

She took them carefully out of the dish and laid them on the sideboard. Each piece would be cut, seasoned, and blended with shallot, sage, breadcrumbs and plenty of salt and pepper.

Lizzie peeled and chopped five shallots. The back door was open, and she could hear the rustling of a fresh, early morning wind in the leaves, the twittering of birds. She hadn't slept much, but it didn't matter. It was a new day.

The dog sniffed around her feet. Lizzie promised a walk.

"Just as soon as this is done, Rita," she crooned. "Just as soon as this is done."

She sliced the organs on the chopping board and mixed them in a large glass bowl with the sage, shallot and seasoning. It was too lumpy for sausages. The mixture went into the blender in three stages. She rolled and shaped the sausages, plopped four in the frying pan, to be eaten with a piece of white bread. The rest went in the fridge.

Accomplishing things, Lizzie was starting to realize, meant putting yourself in the right state of mind. "I thought I could do it," she whispered, "and then I found that I could."

From the cupboard she took a tin of duck confit and warmed it through. She'd looked on the Internet for a good recipe using up lots of offal. In Italy and Spain, to make ends meet, people had started eating shoulder, blood and lung of pig.

Cassoulet de Castelnaudary

100g white haricot beans, presoaked overnight
1 medium onion, stuck with a clove

1 stalk celery, washed

50g carrots, peeled and quartered

1½ tablespoons tomato purée

500g ventrèche salt belly of pork; remove rind and
keep

2 tablespoons duck fat, from confit

2 confit duck legs

350g Lautrec sausages

bouquet garni

1 liter stock

The hip section had fully defrosted in the shed overnight and was now on the kitchen floor, on newspaper. Kneeling beside him with the carving knife, Lizzie sliced four large fillets out of his buttocks. There was dimpling on the skin and a thick layer of white-yellow smelly fat beneath, then flesh—pale pink, like the color underneath an eye. She put the pieces on the sideboard, cubed them like *lardons;* then she sliced five cloves of garlic, two more shallots, and seasoned the mixture in a glass bowl.

She took a small onion from the box in the garage and pierced it with a clove; then she took a stick of celery and three carrots from the fridge. The wind was picking up; she shut the back door. The carrots were washed, peeled and quartered; the celery rinsed. Lizzie wiped her hands on her apron and filled a large saucepan to boil the beans. She waited, tapping her fingernails on the sideboard, and then decided to get to work on the rest of him, cutting more slices of fat from above his hips. She stopped humming and straightened the newspaper under him. The dog was out in the garden, running in circles and barking at trees.

Lizzie got two pristine white tea towels out of the drawer to lay over the wounds on Jacob's hip area. The willy was still to come. Then the testicles, and knowing people ate them made her feel better. She could do them like dumplings, in a quick slick of hot oil. Then add to the cassoulet, or eat as they were. In, out, chew.

She drained the beans. She took the two Tupperware containers of feet and hand stock out of the fridge, and boiled the stock in the casserole dish, adding the beans, garlic, buttock fat, shallots, carrots, onion and celery, with one and a half tablespoons of good tomato purée and bouquet garni: everything except the duck fat, salt and meat. She brought the casserole back up to the boil, then turned the heat down and left it to simmer.

At the sideboard, she removed the sausages in cling film from the fridge. These she quartered and added, with the cuts from his hips, to the beans. Very quickly she bent down to the floor with the carving knife, flipped his hips over, whipped his willy off at the base and plopped it on the chopping board. She pulled his balls away from his body, sliced through the scrotum and tucked these in too. Then she turned him back over and laid the two tea towels over his bits and wounds. She had been jealous of his visits to London to see Joanna. She had felt something when he came back from the Pearl, too. Jacob had gone to the place in Guildford where he could get "a little time and companionship" for one hundred and fifty pounds an hour. They'd not had that kind of money. Not ever. He'd left the card in the glove box of the Volvo and Lizzie had looked online to see a page of lovely-looking young women glancing backwards at the camera with their shiny, smooth bottoms on show. Every single one of them had long hair to the waist. She'd wondered how they got that, how they all managed to have that kind of hair. He'd gone there, once in the first year, then again the next. One hundred and fifty pounds.

"Where've you been?

"Jacob?"

He hadn't said anything, but he hadn't been uppity from it either. He'd slunk back in with his shoulders down, and she had known that whatever he'd gone and done, it had been grim and desperate, and not something he'd enjoyed very much. She had gone out to the garden and buried her hands and feet deep in the soil and the smell of the roses and she had felt self-contained and relieved, in a way, that she'd not had to sink so low, and hadn't ever felt that kind of awful desperation. She'd never needed to romp around to feel alive. She didn't need to romp with Tom Vickory to feel young and desirable either. She'd never, in fact, felt desirable to anyone, which, on balance, was probably a good thing. At least she was going to be able to get away and keep things to herself.

179. Without a shadow of doubt, the most sensible thought you've had all morning.

"You're just not feeling it," Jacob had shouted, once, writhing on top of her, trying to yank her sweater down.
     "I am!" she'd said. "Please! I am."
     The following week she'd asked him if they might try again sometime.
     He'd said, "Of course we can," and put an arm around her; then he'd turned the television on.

180. Passive-aggressives are also master procrastinators. While all of us like to put off unpleasant tasks from time to time, people with passive-aggressive personalities rely on procrastination as a way of frustrating others and/or getting out of certain chores without having to directly refuse them.

181. They can't say, No. But they will make your life al-
     most intolerable while you wait for the yes.
182. Or they will make very sure that you regret ever
     having asked.

Yes, Lizzie had been able to feel it; and it wasn't so far
from the surface as he might have supposed. But it was
buried, she thought, melting the confit, under not feeling very good about herself.

How quickly love shrank into the tiny space it was
given, she thought, as she turned the pieces in the fat
with a dessert spoon. She smoothed her hands on her
apron. She took the cling film from the sausages and
added these to the heavy-bottomed pan where the slices
of his privates were browning in the duck fat. She
opened the back door. She browned, and pushed with
the spoon. Then she tipped the lot into the beans to boil.

Convincing oneself that anything was not just possible but also probable was an excellent way of persuading
the conscious mind that the unconscious was in control.
She smoked in the garden while the beans and the meat
pieces came to the boil, and soon the kitchen was filled
with steam and the smells of garlic and herbs.

Hell it had been, actually, to love a man who couldn't
help himself. How many women all over the world had
done it, though, and not said a word, but carried on
smilingly while behind the scenes, in the spaces be-

tween conversations, between rooms, between what was said and what wasn't, a space was growing, like a sad face slowly coming into view on the wall behind the marital bed.

But what if he hadn't needed saving? What if the problem had been her, and without her he'd just been terribly cheerful? How well he'd bundled out of bed in the morning and bustled about pretending to do things; how cheerfully he'd gone off to the supermarket and come back holding aloft a bottle of wine, or the cheese crackers she'd pointed at once before.

Look at how well he was!

It was her, then.

"I think it's you, Lizzie."

"What is?"

"The problem. To be honest. With drink and every-thing. And the whole attitude to life. I think it's you."

"I don't understand."

"It doesn't matter."

"What doesn't matter?"

"Nothing." Smile. "Nothing at all."

She opened up the laptop and sent an email. It was nearly noon.

Hi, Joanna, it's Lizzie. Are you all right?

She lit a cigarette and placed the lighter upright on the kitchen table. A bead of sweat slid from under her armpit down to her waist. She waited. Her chest was tight. She tried to breathe.

I'm just asking, just thought to say hi, touch base. Don't worry if you're busy. We don't need to talk now. Am sure you're busy.

If she'd come here lost and down on herself and looking for a place to feel at home, she had certainly gained, in addition to that, a feeling that had outgrown the sadness, like ivy growing in a pot of something else. This had become the dominant state of mind, and perhaps it was easier to manage that way, to see the state of unease as being like a monkey to carry about that needed constant soothing. Whereas the sadness was not so easy to feel; it was a constant, colorless thing about being human and getting hurt and losing; in the end it was too much to take in, too much to be close to. So Lizzie had become the frizzy wick striding around the woods in jeans, wringing hands sometimes. Other times she had shrunk into the sofa and gone very quiet. They had picked up each other's moods. It had been impossible not to. Fretfulness had thrived in her from never having had an honest conversation, never quite knowing the whole story, or being able to trust that the man lying beside her was who he said he was.

"What do you think the problem is, Jacob?"

"With what, Lizzie? With who?"

"With me, Jacob. With us."

There wasn't an answer.

There was one person in these woods who'd heard her, who'd seen her, with frustration, years ago, with a big branch she'd broken off a tree, smashing a patch of earth and the bark of another tree. Then he'd seen her again, the same man, whacking the earth up on the common a week ago. More frustration. Nasty old meddlesome man. He suspected her: he knew she was up to something. It was only a matter of days before he came here and knocked on the door.

What do you mean?

Not sure. Just lacking the thing that tells people if they're all right or not, I think. You know?

Can I help?

There was a pause.

I don't know. Are you frightened? Do you ever feel trapped? Like this feeling that you can't get out, or that someone is coming to get you, someone... you know? Like funny smells? I have this thing about smells. I can't stop. I sniff everything, all the time.

Would you like me to come down to see you, Lizzie? I can come this evening. It's honestly fine. I'll be there in a couple of hours. Poss just a little more.

Not today. Not now. No.

*Do you not think Jacob would have wanted me to pop
in and see if you're all right? Especially if you're not?*
I am all right!
He left you, Lizzie!
I know!
It's not your fault.
Yes.
He left you, Lizzie! He left you.
*You're so kind! I don't deserve it. Really don't. Not
good. Not fit for a friend. Heaven knows. Goodbye.*

Lizzie used her long legs and ran into the garden. She
left the back door open and the dog came running after her. She bounded over the mud on the turfed-up
lawn and leaped over the wall. She cracked twigs un-
derfoot and pushed through the bracken. She stumbled
over branches, heard the dog bark. She wasn't the gentle pale woman who slipped out of things anymore, but
a tougher thing of bone and sinew smashing through
the woods. Everywhere she looked there was dark and
damp; and dripping, seething, slimy wood life growing
over cracks and dark and green moss.

She tripped and fell, got up and pushed herself to
run faster, thumping her stomach with her hand as she
went. Fifty-five, and a garden spade.

What was left for her, then, was the moment-by-mo-
ment construction of a life without feeling, of not, for
one moment, holding an eye; of not looking at that

which would show her what it was to be base, which was cruelty, and hatefulness, of a deep, terrifying, battering rage that came out of nowhere and turned on its own. She had failed to civilize. She had not known enough, had enough, to become gracious and elegant and wise. Now there was only life left living on the edge, eking something out that felt manageable without feeling. That was it now, forever.

Lizzie ran through the trees and burst into an open field where she kept her mouth shut and the air in as she ran, feeling her lungs constrict as she tried not to breathe. She ran through the wet grass, flicking mud behind her heels, and didn't stop for the stitch in her side or the aching breasts juddering in an old, gray bra. She pushed forward with her thigh muscles and with her neck, and with her lips pursed and all the blood filling her face so that she looked truly mad, truly red with human blood and rage and a stomach full of her husband's flesh, and behind her, excited, the dog ran and barked and together they made it up onto the common where Lizzie fell down and sat, straight-legged, back on the thin grass.

It was over. It was too much. It had beaten her. Of course it had. The only thing she could do now was go home and get in the car and drive to the police station in Farnham and wait to be seen.

She would walk in, up the steps, past the little blue lamp on the right side of the door, and take a seat in the waiting room. There was no rush, after all; it certainly wasn't an emergency and there was nothing she'd be able to do about the people in the future screaming her name.

She'd go to prison for the rest of her life, and it wouldn't matter what anyone did to her there. They could spit and kick and beat and punch. They could come at night and knife her in the side while she was sleeping. What did it matter? Of course she wouldn't be able to use her skills as a practical person to make life better for herself there. Sooner or later there would come a time when she was ready to die, but doing that to herself now, committing suicide, and leaving half of him in the freezer, and the back door open with the dog wandering around, seemed not just silly, and selfish, and messy for everyone to cope with, but far too frightening, requiring will and energy she was sure she didn't have.

The neighbors would want an explanation; Nic would come back and she and Mike would want to know about the woman behind their cake, and poor Tom Vickory, who'd sat in the kitchen with Jacob Prain's heart in the oven, would need to be told something, would need to have someone who could explain.

I've come to make a confession, she'd say to the woman at the desk. I've come to confess a crime. Whereupon the woman at the desk would most likely roll her eyes and take in the white face and jeans and the waxed green jacket and turn to her colleague, also at the desk, and mutter something only the two of them would be able to understand. They'd have a code word. So many people came in with wringing hands and a sense of guilt these days. So many people out of work and wondering what to do with their lives. People getting stuck and fighting with each other, smashing things, or quietly, meanly, turning away. And Lizzie would be standing there knowing she'd murdered him, knowing she'd eaten him, and was waiting now to tell this to the woman with the orange face and rolling eyes whose colleague was leaning over helping someone who'd lost her bag or had it nicked to fill in a form, and Lizzie would have to wait to tell them. She'd killed her husband one morning in March and had eaten most of him.

They would say: Wait! What would they do? Who would call the supervisor? Would it suddenly get very hot in the police station, very hot, very strained? Would it go quiet, or loud? How long before she was cuffed? Would the lights go out around the station as people inside tried to keep calm?

183. You have eaten an awful lot of protein.
184. Symptoms of a protein overdose include: abdominal cramps, constipation, and mental disturbance.

185. It is therefore understandable that, fearing loss of your mind, you have whittled your options down to (a) suicide, or (b) confession.

186. Nothing has changed from where you were before. You are doing well, safe in your little world—house, garden, woodland isolation, fire in the evenings, bottle of wine with your meal—before you reached out and tried to make a friend.

187. There is also an option (c).

188. You can do nothing.

189. Go home now and have a quiet day. Sit out in the garden with a cup of coffee and a cigarette, and run yourself a nice bath. Get some much-needed sleep. In the morning, you will feel ready to get on.

It had begun to drizzle with rain. It was the afternoon. There was darkness and then there was light. Each moment could be isolated. She saw the cows in the distance, and spoke softly, calling the dog's name.

She tugged the collar of her coat up against the cold and went round the edges of the field. Images of Jacob as he had been in the beginning, gentle with her, nice to her, came in like butterflies and disappeared. Thought didn't cling to the images—and her head was without voices. She wouldn't be going to Scotland. She wouldn't need to eat anymore. The car would get her to the police station and she would walk on in. It felt better. She kicked the ground with her boot. She put her hands in the pockets of her coat, then took them out and folded them across her breasts.

She looked at the cows, and the church spire in the distance. It was a wet, gray day, but the countryside around here was beautiful. The dog scurried and dashed about with its tongue lolling pink and huge from its sopping mouth.

This was freedom. This was what it felt like.

She closed her eyes.

She watched the dog and felt very quiet in the air at the top of the field. Her decision was made. She took a deep breath and whispered her relief to the clouds on the horizon. She stood up and put her hands in her pockets. Then she backtracked into the woods, going a different path to get home. She felt like a different person. She'd let go of the struggle, she'd surrendered to prudence and now her conscience might make a tentative return.

She was almost at the farm. She cut through the trees and joined Tubford Lane, turning left to walk the distance home. There were bumps and puddles in the lane. She saw two bikes disappearing round the bend ahead of her, and she peered into the gray light after them.

The car was up ahead in the lane, parked as usual, where it had been for years. The piece of paper had been taped to the back windscreen, with masking tape, the black-and-white picture was grainy, but Jacob's face and form were clear. He was grinning, with his teeth exposed. She put a hand out to the boot and leaned her weight against it as she stared at the pitiful poster and the photograph of her husband. She read the word: MISSING. Then underneath that, printed in red: CIRCUMSTANCES MYSTERIOUS AND POSSIBLY SINISTER.

Lizzie ripped the paper off the back of the car. She went into the house through the front door and walked in her boots to the kitchen, crushing the paper and tape into a sticky ball. She pushed it far down into the bin with the onion skins and the carrot peelings and the haricot beans she hadn't used. In the garage she fed the dog and filled the bowl with clean water. Then she sat at the kitchen table carefully peeling the skin from an apple with a fruit knife.

¶

190. Book an appointment at the hairdresser's.
191. Resolve to take all your money out of the joint account and close it down.
192. Close down his email account. Close down your own.
193. You've done so well. You're nearly there. Soon everything will be empty and tidy and you can start all over again!
194. Even at the end of the world.

195. Do not think, btw, that you have come to the end of the world.
196. You haven't.
197. You're all right, Lizzie Prain. You're going to be all right.

The left arm and the right arm went into the microwave, one after the other. She shaved them on the sideboard and then bent them on the baking tray so that they looked like boomerangs. She lifted one off and tried fitting it into the microwave in an acute triangle. Between wrist and shoulder stump there wasn't much. It would work. She took the joint back out to prepare it.

She was in her apron again, oven on, radio on. She cracked black pepper, sprinkled salt. She sloshed with olive oil and tucked some garlic cloves underneath the elbow joints. She chopped an onion and threw it on: five minutes in the microwave, ping, then into the oven, and from the freezer she lifted the remaining thigh.

Out in the garden she chopped with the axe. The bits of thigh were split in two. Each could go in the microwave, like the arms, pale, stuffed in; the microwave would be useless after all this: it could be thrown on the bonfire and exploded with a bit of meths and a match.

Boom!

She wiped the kitchen surfaces with the lemon spray till all was sparkly clean. On the sideboard the bits of thigh were piled up under a tea towel.

She took his arms from the oven and cut them into the rings she'd make of a baguette, using the serrated edge of the bread knife. The hairs had singed; they stank. Even the marrow inside his bones would be eaten now she was back in the mood; and there wouldn't be any more thinking of silly things like running off to the police station to tell someone, or reaching out to make friends.

She was absolutely back on course. And she knew that her eyes were fixed open; she wasn't blinking. She'd ripped that poster off the car.

She sat at the table and ate the meat, using a steak knife to cut the flesh from his upper arms away from the bone, and then using a teaspoon to scoop out the funny-tasting marrow, which was a little muddy, and dry.

Lizzie sat for one and a half hours and chewed what was in her mouth, and swallowed. Then she went upstairs to lie down.

She slipped under the duvet in all of her clothes, and she lay very still, on her back, and stared at the ceiling for a while. Oak, he'd wanted. For its longevity and rotund glory. A tree that would go on when he was gone. The garden and its trees growing down in the dark by the wall would be there after she'd left. So early, and he'd been out already. Trying to dig a hole. In the frost. She'd got dressed into the clothes she'd been wearing all weekend. Nothing new bought for years. No linen trousers, no nice shoes. Nothing like Joanna. Through to the kitchen. Because of the job? Because of Joanna? Because of the cakes? Because of the Pearl? Because she hadn't had the imagination to get away? Bringing the spade down on the back of his head. Then the small mental adjustment. Doing it again. Nothing. Like a car crash. She'd turned him over, slipped on the grass, his head had lolled in the hole; she'd hauled it back up, and tried to pull him down at the feet and straighten him out on the grass.

There was meat to eat. She would have to press her mouth against a wall of cold thigh.

She lay there retching, and she curled on her side.

There was still all this to go.

"I am sorry," she said, and she heard the words come right out.

One could learn to be alive.

She'd put the last of the bones and fat in the stockpot with bouquet garni and celery. She would need the clothes peg on again while it boiled and simmered and this she would do with candles burning before she went to bed, and reduce it with wine, then blend again, reduce for an hour more till she got a stock which could be stored. She had to keep going. And ignore what sounded to her like repeated knocks on the front door. A little scratching at the bathroom window. Only wind, she thought. Only trees.

There would be a final meal.

Lizzie Prain chopped her husband into bits.

They had been an isolated couple.

Living quietly.

In the Surrey Hills.

Five minutes from the A31 to Farnham.

It's an Area of Outstanding Natural Beauty.

The cushions on the garden chairs had been there Lizzie's whole lifetime.

They'd been bought by his aunt.

They'd listened to the news on the radio, not having a subscription or being members of a newspaper readership. Or members of anything at all.

Not that she'd wanted it.

Not from the sofa. With the television on. And not feeling anything for him. How could she have felt anything for him?

Though it might have been nice to meet some people.

It might have been nice.

She blinked, and she understood that it was mechanical. There was nothing to fear. She would go north on the train, after that frozen emotional state—one movement at a time.

Tom

She came back from Scotland on Thursday. I'd been there since Sunday. I came back from work that night and saw that the lights were on. At first I thought it might have been her husband returned from abroad. I put my bike up against the yew hedge and went in.

The dog was sniffing around in the hall. I stepped into the kitchen and saw the bags there, by the back door. The cool bag was open and it was full of sopping, stinking newspaper and polythene. I didn't want to go near it. Even Rita recoiled. She barked and growled, sat back on her haunches, then leaped forward and backed away. I called out for Lizzie. I didn't go out to the garden and I felt sure that she wasn't in the house. I assumed she'd gone for a walk in the lane or popped up to the pub for a drink, so I took the box of pizza I'd brought, and then went into the living room with a book. There wasn't anything in that room but the old sofa and a fireplace. I'd been using the fire in the evenings.

While I was sitting in the living room the back door to the kitchen opened and banged shut. I heard her washing her hands at the sink. I knew it was her, without having to look round, so I simply stayed where I was, with an unchewed bit of pizza in my mouth.

All of a sudden I felt very scared. I can't honestly explain where the feeling came from, but it was real and had no thought attached to it. It was as if my heart just stopped for a beat or two, and my nervous system was flooded with adrenaline.

I stood up and turned round as she came into the room.

"I've dug a hole in the flower bed, Tom," she said, without even saying hi or explaining why she'd come back. She was smiling. Her face was shining with sweat. She looked almost pretty, and very bright.

I said: "Oh, right. OK."

"And tomorrow I'd like us to plant a tree!"

Her voice was very forced; her smile was wide and seemed to be stuck there.

I offered her a slice of pizza. She came on over to the sofa, picked up a slice, and sat down beside me. Her boots were muddy and old. I could smell the soil on her. I didn't want to ask about the cool bag. I thought that she'd had some food and forgotten about it on the train. Something had gone off, and in her hurry to get back she hadn't noticed. It wasn't like her to be like that. She was such a clean and hygienic, practical sort of woman. But she was acting strange. I wanted to ask what had happened up there to bring her home.

"Have you had a good day?" she said, turning very deliberately on the sofa to look at me. She folded her hands and placed them demurely in her lap.

She said how much warmer it was in the south of England than it had been in Scotland.

"Did the men come to take the freezer?" she said.

I said that they hadn't turned up. "I called them but no one answered the phone. It didn't go to voicemail so I couldn't leave a message."

Lizzie turned around again, sat back against the sofa, but was still very erect. She looked around, and sniffed the air, as if she had never sat on that sofa or breathed the air in that room.

"How strange that they didn't come," she said, and then she turned to me with that fixed bright smile again.

"I could ring them tomorrow," I said.

"No matter," she said. "I will."

"Maybe they felt they couldn't get the lorry up the lane. Maybe they came and tried. It's muddy down at the bottom there. And bumpy."

"They wouldn't have come in a lorry too big to fit down the lane. I said it was small, quite tight. With overhanging branches. I said it would be a job."

"I'm sure they'll come," I said, and I went for another slice of pizza.

I didn't ask her how Scotland had been. It was obvious it hadn't been great. I looked at those small, very round, slightly panicky blue eyes, so close together, like the eyes of a doll.

"I'm not asking for anything," she said. "You can stay here with me or you can go. It's entirely up to you."

I said nothing. I just looked at her and smiled.

"It's perfectly all right. Tom?"

I smiled again, and I felt my whole face crinkling with it and my heart leaped into my mouth with apprehension for her, for us, for everything. She could feel it too. She sat back. I saw her shoulders drop. After a while she took a very deep breath, and then collapsed back into the sofa.

"I can stay in the shed," I suggested. "If that would be easier?"

She shrugged. "Don't be silly. The shed!"

"But you said before you thought it was a good idea. It is. It'll be great! I'm sure I'll like it!"

"It's fine," she said. "Just stay in the house."

We said nothing much else that night. We finished the pizza and then we sat in the warmth of the fire, and we made cups of tea to take upstairs. I had my book. Lizzie wanted to lie down on the mattress and sleep. She brushed her teeth. I brought a blanket up. I opened up my sleeping bag and put it over both of us. She didn't say a word. We were still in all our clothes. I put my arm under my head and I lay there for a while with my book while she fell asleep.

13

Once the potatoes had boiled, Lizzie ran up the lane towards the farm. If she ran, she felt, she would work up an appetite for his head. It had been defrosting overnight in the small space at the front of the shed—and the shed stank, so she'd left the door open and would need to go in there later in the afternoon and give it a good dousing with bleach.

She came to the farmhouse and crunched across the gravel, past the two saloon cars both spattered with mud, and up to the front door. She knocked. There was nothing. She knocked again. Inside someone was calling. One of the twins came to the door and opened it a crack.

Lizzie stood on the front step with her shoulders hunched. The door opened a little more. Lizzie could see a bony shoulder in a pale pink vest, a hip protruding from gray tracksuit bottoms.

"Are you Claire?" said Lizzie, placing her foot just inside the door so as to ease it open a little.

"Hi," said the girl. She called back into the house. "Mum!"

There wasn't a response. Lizzie looked beyond the girl

into the wide hallway of the house. She remembered doing the babysitting here and thought about how people
could go to a new experience happily, bounding forward,
full of hope. She had been like that too. She had felt
uncomfortable, but she had quite liked the challenge.
Though they had thought her weird. She could have
found someone to help. She could have gone to see a
therapist of some description, or made a friend. There
would have been someone to talk to, wouldn't there?

"Are you Claire, then?" she said, her eye on the foot of
hers that was now wedging open the door. She straightened up and folded her hands, nun-like, in front of her
waist.

"Yeah. I'm Claire. Nic's not back yet. She's back
tonight. Mike's here. He's upstairs. Do you want to
speak to him?"

"Actually, I'd like to speak to your grandad," said
Lizzie.

The girl looked at her watch. "Still asleep," she said.

A black Labrador slid around the girl's legs and
bounded down the steps. Claire said, "Ralph." The dog
went on.

Claire grimaced. Lizzie turned and watched the dog
bound across the grass and down towards the pool of
muddy water around the fence to the field. She wouldn't
have to do this again. She wouldn't have to be here anymore. There was only the head left. Then she was free.

"It's just that I found one of his signs yesterday," she

said. "It was taped to the back of my car. Could you tell him please that my husband left me and eloped to South America with a woman from the Pearl. It's in Guildford. Do you know it?"

Claire was looking at her fingernails.

"It's a prostitute place," said Lizzie. "Where people go for—"

"Yeah, I get it," said the girl.

"Obviously, it's my own private matter, and I don't appreciate being stalked..."

"Grandad's not exactly well," said Claire. "I'll tell Mum and everything and we'll definitely make sure it doesn't happen again, but don't worry. He's not all there."

"Does he find it funny?"

"No. He's just not sure."

"Not sure?"

"Of himself. Or anything. Of where he is. Who belongs where. Guess he thinks like he's alive and trying to mix with people somehow. Trying to...don't know."

"Does he stay in his room most days?"

"Most days. He comes out when it's quiet. Like once or twice a month he goes for a walk. Or goes to the pub. Sometimes he gets lost. He's in his own head. Can be hard to keep tabs on him."

There was a pause.

She turned back into the house again and shouted for her mum.

Mum didn't come.

Claire looked like she wanted to go in and wanted to find something to say to please.

"I like your jumper," she said.

Lizzie wasn't sure she'd heard her. It was as if her senses had become precisely and finely tuned now to getting only what she needed. It was cold, and ever so slightly exciting. It was her determination now— her wits—being tested against the world. It was as if her own head—in preparation for eating his—had become detached from her body, and she was up now, in the clear, clean, cold air, enough of her money in her wallet to get her away from here and into a new life, and fuck everyone else. Yeah. And she liked that feeling.

Then Tom came to the door, slinking up behind his sister, in a T-shirt and jeans. His cheeks were still bright red; his eyes darting a little in their sockets.

Claire slid away and Tom was standing there, six foot two with a bit of tissue on a bleeding spot on his neck.

Lizzie smiled. She said: "Hiya."

"Hi," he said, shyly. "I've been thinking about the shed. Can I come tonight?"

Lizzie paused.

"To look at the shed?" he said. He put a hand on his stomach and two tears popped out of his eyes.

"Man!" he said. "What is it with you?"

Lizzie backed away.

"Don't worry," she said, lifting a flat palm up in the air like a policeman. "I'm going anyway. It doesn't matter what happens."

"No, wait!"

He came after her, ankles creaking. He wasn't wearing shoes. They stood in a thin patch of sunlight on the gravel driveway.

"I want to come and help you clear the shed," he said. "Please. Let me come and help?"

198. You are now in the final stages.
199. This is excellent.
200. Say to yourself: I am a remarkable woman.
201. Say no to Tom Vickory if his intentions are more than clearing out the shed with you.
202. Having him round this evening, whatever you intend to serve him for supper, could jeopardize your chances of ever getting out.
203. Think what it might do to the poor boy if he ever knew.

She got the head from the shed and brought it into the kitchen and put it down on newspaper on the floor. She took the twisty off the bin liner and peeled the label off. She reached into the bag and pulled his head out, cradling it against her stomach with the plastic underneath it to prevent any loose hairs dropping off him and onto the floor. She felt the cool wet slime against her stomach. It had passed through her apron and was seeping through her shirt. Her pale yellow apron from the farm shop in Seale would have to go in the wash now. She would put it on a hot wash and leave it out on the line to dry while she was gone.

She ran her hand down the back of his head and drew an imaginary line where an incision would be made with an axe.

She would get the brain out, cook it in the oven, eat it for lunch and then think about what to do with the rest. The cheeks could be cut away easily and fried as they were in the frying pan, and the eyes could be used, also, taken out with a knife and blanched in a little oil. Or steamed, wrapped in a lettuce parcel. She ran her fingers round to the front of his head on her stomach and made sure that the lids were closed. She felt the matted hair. She closed her eyes and trembled. She tried to imagine that she was holding a sculpted head in her hands, and then it was simply a matter of chipping away at the bits she needed.

"Fine," she said, and she took a breath. There was no sound in the kitchen. Rita was running round and round the garden. Inside the house it was only her. She wasn't afraid.

Out on the grass she took the axe high in the air and thwacked it down on the back of his skull.

Jacob's head split open in two clean pieces and Lizzie bent down with the carving knife to cut out his brain. It was easier than she'd thought it would be. She peered down and found the inside of his head very pink, very delicate, some white in places: not an awful lot to see. The brain was distinctive: snug in its socket, it was exactly like a piece of white coral, with the consistency of toothpaste when she touched it, and much smaller than she'd imagined.

She scooped the brain out with a spoon and tipped it into a small ceramic roasting dish. The dog barked and trotted after her as she carried the dish back into the kitchen. Then she put it in the oven with nothing at all to go with it. There was milk in the fridge, and Lizzie felt compelled, suddenly, to pour the milk into his head and then press the two bits of his skull together, filling him back up somehow, correcting the difficulties he'd grown up with, the ways in which he'd let himself down. Something to do with the whiteness of milk, not the symbolic significance, but the taste of it, how soothing it was, made her want to pour it into his head. Instead she pressed the two pieces of his skull back together, then wrapped him back up in the bin liner, tied it with a twisty and went out to the fine rain in the garden, where she stood holding it under one arm and looked at the trees.

After a while she perched at the outside table. She sat for a few minutes and did not reach a conclusion.

She listened to the sound of the woods and willed her thoughts out into the trees. After she had done this, thoughts would come and they would drive her mad.

She put the head down on the table and left it there while she went back into the kitchen to check on the brain.

She looked at her watch. The brain had cooked. It didn't smell. It had gone a pale golden color, and when she pressed it, it felt firm, slightly crisp at the edges. She put it back in the oven. It might work with some soy sauce. If she crisped it up a little more in her small frying pan, it would be like eating a pile of crispy noodles.

She heated sesame oil in the pan and broke the brain up with a fork while it fried. She used a slotted spoon to transfer it onto a plate and ripped off a sheet of kitchen roll. She sat down at the table with a glass of wine. It was the last of the fourth bottle from the fridge. That was fine. It was perfect. She took a bite. The brain had a bitter flavor, something very deep and pungent—a grainy texture, but nicely crispy and salty on the outside.

She ate his brain in ten mouthfuls. Then she washed everything up in the sink. The head was still on the outside table in its bag. Lizzie looked through the kitchen window at it, and then she gave up trying to think about how to make eating the rest of it easier for herself. There wasn't an answer. So she put it back in the freezer and piled the garden cushions up on top. Upstairs she brushed her teeth, had a shower, and dried herself with the only towel she had left. Then she lay down on her bed and placed her hands on her chest.

Tom

I hadn't done anything about the three little sculptures she found at the back of the shed. She was so tense and tired when she came in from the garden that first night that she didn't even notice them. She'd given me the number of a woman in London to call, but I didn't think there was any rush so they were still there on the kitchen table.

I don't know much about art, but even I could see that they were nice—and that they'd been made by someone who'd been "present" in himself and with his gifts at the time of creation. There was definitely an energy in each of the little sculptures, but I never imagined that they would make as much money as Joanna went on to get for them. It was Joanna who got in touch with me by email, months afterwards, to let me know that they had sold. No one would have thought it would work out like that. Not of this guy who just lived out in the woods and made the odd piece from time to time. I'd moved up north by then and I'd lost touch with everyone. In her email Joanna said that she would try to track Jacob down to let him know about the sale. "I think Lizzie really underestimated his talent," she said. Of course I would never reply.

"You're a funny one, Tom," Lizzie said when she woke up next to me on the first morning back from Scotland, and stretched her arms out. We were lying on the mattress on the floor. She stretched her arms back and looked at the trees.

"I could say the same for you," I said. "You're still in all your clothes from the train."

"Funny One Tom," she said.

We were both a little awkward, and being friendly, cheery, polite.

"Today I'm going to plant a tree in the flower bed," she said. "And then I'm going to go and get a job."

"Why?"

"Because it's possible I'll be all right here. If I like the job then I will stay."

She was speaking very matter-of-factly, and there was this strange sense of excitement about her. I mentioned the figurines, and that I hadn't done anything with them, and then I reminded her about the freezer.

I took up my book and pretended to read a little more. I was too bewildered by her return and her excitement. I remember feeling really hot. And then suddenly really cold. I closed my eyes again and let all the feelings of warmth and confusion and cold and comfort and loss move through me until Lizzie got up in her jumper and jeans and went through to the bathroom. Then I sat bolt upright and went to the window to open it for some air.

We had breakfast, but not together. We were both used to having toast and coffee standing up, while fiddling around in the kitchen, and that's what we did the first morning. Even though it was still quite cold we both preferred to have the back door open and to stand there in jumpers letting in the fresh air. I stood at the kitchen window and looked at the shed; I knew it was only a matter of days before she would ask me to move in there, whatever she had said the night before about me being free to stay or go. This was her home. It had been her home for decades. She wasn't just going to start sharing it with a total stranger, I thought. Even if she was a woman feeling alone.

"I cleared the shed out, and I swept it," I said to her.

Lizzie looked at the pieces standing on the table.

"I'm going to invite the woman who wants them. In a few days I'll ask her to come here. You can meet her, Tom. I think we'll both find her glamorous. And you'll be able to help me work out if she genuinely wants to be my friend or if she's only interested in getting her hands on these."

"It's one of life's lessons," I said, and Lizzie squinted at me.

"What is?"

"Knowing who you can trust," I said, and swallowed

the toast. She was still on edge. Blimey, she was on edge. I felt a bit weird again. I wasn't sure if I was going to be able to stand it.

She said she'd come with me to the garden center when I went for the early shift. I wanted to go on my bike, because I really needed the fresh air. To start with she drove behind me, going really slowly on the main road. Then I pulled over onto the verge and waved her on. I saw the driver's window come down and a hand come out with a thumb pointing upwards, and it made me laugh.

When I got there, Lizzie was waiting for me, just standing in the fog at the entrance with her bag.

She bought a tiny oak tree. I helped her to put the tree in the back of the car with the pot on its side and the back seats down. It went very easily into the boot—and Lizzie drove it home while I stayed behind to work.

She said she spent all day digging the hole, digging as far down into the flower bed as it was possible to go. She hadn't put the tree in yet. I looked down into the hole. She had certainly made it bigger. She had been working on it for six hours. There was fresh earth and compost from the flower bed in the bottom of it.

"The sun came through in the end," she said, and there was mud on her face. "It turned into a nice day. Thanks for the new tools," she added. She had her foot resting on her spade. "Great spade, Tom."

"I've still got the receipt," I said, fishing my wallet out

from my back pocket. "I got a discount on them but they were still quite a lot."

"Will you help me put the oak tree in, please, Tom?"

We lifted it up and we nestled it down into the hole. I felt it press onto the pile of new earth she had put down there and I imagined the roots growing into the soft dark earth.

I asked her why she had gone so deep into the ground. A tree sapling didn't need to go nearly that far down.

"I realized that," she said, taking a deep breath. Then she said she'd had a lovely afternoon.

"I think it's nice that you're here, Tom. Everything feels lighter. And sunnier."

I shrugged and asked if I could smoke one of her cigarettes as we went back inside. That wasn't like me. I was off kilter. We were trying too hard.

"I've made us some supper," she said, and she lifted the lid of the saucepan so that I could smell the cinnamon and cloves.

It was the nicest rice and vegetable dish that I have ever tasted. I sat down with her at the kitchen table, and I ate the food and we didn't say much to each other, but soon we were both feeling a bit more relaxed.

"I rang the freezer men," she said. "They're going to come tomorrow."

"Be nice to have it clear," I said. "Shame Mike and Nic haven't come back to you. I thought they were keen."

"It's quite all right," she said, in a way that made me realize it wasn't.

"It'll work out," I said.

"Who will take it on, Tom? What will they be like?"

I laughed and messed around, pretending to hold a crystal ball.

"I see man and woman. Funny man with long hair. Skeeny woman. They want to have child. Child will bring healing to sad hearts."

I looked at her and could see the emotion she was struggling with in her face. I told her that I thought turning the garage into a games room for kids was a good idea.

"A family with young kids would be great," she said. "See what the house wants." She was teasing me, and raising her eyes in a way that suggested she'd said something spooky. She didn't want to be spooky. She didn't want to freak me out. She wanted to go to Scotland. And she wanted to be all right in her own home. She wanted to be liked by me. I'm still not sure I fully understand why. So I changed the subject.

"Are you going to move to Scotland permanently?" I asked her.

"Yes," she said. "When I am ready."

"How long do you think that will be?"

"I don't know, Funny One," she said. "I'm going to wait and see."

Everything about that house spoke to me of surrender.

From the roof slightly giving in around the chimney to the way the windows didn't quite meet in the bedroom. Things had bent and warped and got damp and I'd started to love that, and to feel myself settling into the softness of it, letting everything breathe.

We ate in silence for the rest of the meal. I tried to make jokes from time to time, which then needed explaining. It wasn't the end of the world.

The most important thing, I felt, was trying not to worry about what I was doing there. Sometimes it came up.

"Do you want me to stay here with you, Lizzie?" I asked her the following morning when we were standing together washing up at the sink.

"I want you to do what you want to do," she said. And then she went up for a bath.

Lizzie went back to the hotel to ask if the job was still available. I encouraged her to do that. She said how grateful she was that I had put her in touch with them. She said that maybe it might just work.

"Shall I go as I am, Tom?" she said, and she smiled in a way that scrunched her cheeks right up to her eyes.

"As you are," I said.

She simply took the dog, walked up the hill, and walked into the hotel lobby.

She told me that the people she'd seen before, Lynn and Steven, were sitting in the tub chairs by the entrance and that they were having coffee, as if they hadn't moved in the three weeks since her interview. "Hi," they both said in unison. "Come to work for us after all?"

They all stood up to shake hands.

Inexplicably, she said, they just seemed to really like her. She told them she was really sorry she hadn't been in touch. Something had happened that she hadn't foreseen and there was nothing she could have done about it. It wasn't a problem, they said. They were still doing interviews. They asked if she would like to give it a go for a week or two, on a trial basis, and see how they got on.

"They were so nice to me, Tom. They were just so very kind."

"People are nice," I said. "They really can be." Which was when she took the packet of cigarettes and went to stand in the garden for an hour.

The freezer men were due to come with the lorry the following day. Everything was going well, Lizzie said, climbing onto the mattress that night, again in all her clothes. I told her I could easily get another mattress from up at the farm, and that we really didn't have to lie side by side in all our clothes.

Lizzie said it was fine, and for the whole of our week together we slept like that.

14

Lizzie parked the car up behind the old cinema and walked with her basket down North Street. The dog had been walked and fed, and the freezer was empty now apart from the head without a brain in its bag, and the two packets of frozen vegetables. She had thought to put the head out with the rubbish—double-bound in a refuse sack and in among the vegetable peelings and the contents of old jars she'd cleaned out of the kitchen cupboards—and leave it for the bin men when they came up the lane in their truck on Wednesday morning. But the image of his head being crushed in the teeth of the truck changed her mind. She went out to the garden and stood for a long time looking at the flower bed by the shed.

Tom was going to take care of things when Lizzie was gone. She couldn't leave anything for him to find, not a speck. And since she couldn't find a way to eat or burn Jacob's lips and cheeks and the eyes that had looked at her for thirty years, it remained her responsibility, and therefore the best thing to do, she felt, was to take the head with her in a cool bag, with ice inside, to keep it frozen on the train. She would need to find a place to rent straightaway; and it wasn't going to be easy. She would have to be alone, not sharing a flat as she might have wanted to, and a bed and breakfast, as a stopgap, wasn't going to be an option. It was an unexpected turn, but one she was going to have to live with. And so she forced herself to accept that, and she made herself sleep with her body lying flat and her hands folded on her chest.

The house was clean. The trainers with blood on them had been through the wash. Everything had been washed, and rinsed, and bleached. She had lit a candle on the kitchen table first thing this morning and it burned as she got changed, switching the thick woolen jumper for a clean shirt and the interview suit she was wearing to go out.

In Guildford, she started with a cappuccino, and sat outside a café where the sun was out on the pavement. It wasn't at all warm; there was an icy wind coming in from somewhere, but Lizzie felt good to be out in the world, and she took her jotter out of her basket and looked through her list.

All that was left for her to do was call the hotel and turn down the job. "I'm so sorry," she rehearsed. "It's just that I've decided to leave the area and start my life again somewhere else."

Then she would clear the last bits from the shed, leave a note for Tom, and send a final email to Joanna, explaining that she was quite all right now, that she felt she was through the turbulence of the past weeks, and was happy to be moving on.

Life did go on. She finished her coffee, took pleasure in the tinkling sound of the spoon on the saucer outside the café on the pavement, and she left some money on the table. She walked into the bank and asked to withdraw five hundred pounds from the joint account.

The first thing she bought was an extra-large cool bag from the camping shop.

"How much would you expect to pay," she asked the woman in the flower shop, "to rent a two-bedroom cottage with a big garden in the woods?"

"All year round?" the woman asked. She pulled some pearls out from the gap in her starched collar and squeezed round behind the desk. "Round here? Detached? Garden? Two grand. You'd be surprised," said the woman, "what people will pay round here for a detached house and bit of land."

Lizzie said nothing. She knew people wouldn't pay that much, not for a damp little place on the bend under the trees.

"I think half that," Lizzie said.

"You just never know," said the woman, as if reading her mind. "People don't see it the way you do."

Lizzie frowned.

"I can see you're thinking you'll never get that much and it'll never rent out, because right now you don't like living there much—why would you? We don't if we're miserable. But things change and you'll look on it differently in time. You'll look back," she said, tugging on her pearls, "and you won't think, 'Golly, what a dump, it'll never sell and never rent.' You'll just think, it is what it is: a cottage, two bedrooms, with a garden in the woods. Sounds lovely."

Lizzie looked at the woman and clutched hold of her bag.

"Sounds like the sort of place an artist would want to live. Or a young couple with a family. Sounds ideal. All that space they can run around in undisturbed. Bet you have an open fire, don't you?"

"Yes."

"See?"

"See what?" said Lizzie.

"It's nicer already, isn't it? Nicer than you thought. Lucky you. Detached house with a big garden in the woods and an open fire. Sounds like heaven, matter of fact. Sounds like you should be counting your blessings, dear."

"I'm going to Scotland," said Lizzie. She turned to pick up a bunch of closed orange tulips. "I'm soon to leave. My husband died."

The woman stretched her fingers out towards the bunch.

"Oh, I am sorry," she said, and tilted her head to the side as if she couldn't quite take it in through both ears. Then she looked at Lizzie like someone who had been trained in the art of extending sympathy without having to participate in the emotion. Like a nurse.

Right at that moment the tears sprang into Lizzie's eyes. She made an effort to speak through the blur.

"Many people choose to live round here, don't they?"

"Didn't you?"

"Yes," said Lizzie. "I came here to study. At the art college in Farnham. Then I met my husband, and stayed."

"Right you are. I was born in Farnborough," the woman said, breathing deeply in through her nose while wrapping the tulips in brown paper and tying them with raffia. Lizzie handed over four pound coins.

"People seem to like their houses painted gray now, don't they? Or just one color throughout. White everywhere. Or gray."

"I like gray," said the woman. "Gray walls. White skirting and ceilings and timber. Wood floors. Flowers everywhere. Different strokes..." she said.

"Yes," said Lizzie, and carried on standing there, unsure as to whether the conversation was finished and she could go.

"Let me take your number," said the woman. "In case I hear of anyone wanting to move. Maybe I will find the person who rents it. Or buys it, should you decide to sell."

"I hadn't thought of that."

"It might turn out to be the right thing," said the woman.

"Thank you," said Lizzie, and she turned in the shop clutching her flowers and her bag and she stepped out into the sunlight on the street.

204. Walk into the hairdresser's and wait to be seen.
205. Try not to look like someone who has been cutting her own hair for many years.
206. You have just as much right to be here as anyone else. Ignore the rumblings in your stomach and explain that you booked an appointment.
207. If you feel suddenly sluggish, try to remember that you are (a) out of your comfort zone, and (b) digesting a brain.
208. Try not to dwell unnecessarily on this. Or make it more than it needs to be.
209. You will be shown to a chair and a young man or woman will enfold you in a black gown. They will ask if you'd like a coffee while you wait. Magazines will be put on the ledge beneath your mirror. Your attention will be drawn to a man or woman across the way who will be coming, in just a second, to cut your hair.

210. Don't worry if the stylist lifts your hair away from your head and looks at it as if it might be straw.
211. Explain that you're not entirely sure what you want but that you would like something new.

At "Bob's" garage in Elstead, Lizzie got out of the car and walked straight into the lean-to office where Bob was sitting watching television on a miniature set. She said, in a voice that was deeper than her own:

"How much will you give me for the car, Bob?"

Bob was wearing a boilersuit stained with grease. He stood up at once and folded his hands on his stomach. He looked out of the window. "Couple a hundred quid," he said.

"I'll bring it to you tomorrow," said Lizzie. "And you can have it for one hundred and fifty quid plus a lift to the station."

"No problem," he said. "Which one you leaving from?"

"Guildford," said Lizzie. "And I need to be there by half-nine."

Lizzie drove home, and looked at herself and her new hair in the rearview mirror. They had left it curly and cut it into a neat little bob around her ears. Then the girl had run some product through it to make it smooth and shiny. It smelled nice, and made Lizzie feel different. No one had mentioned the gray. Once home, she whistled to the dog, grabbed a handful of biscuits from the garage, and off they went to the dump with the axe and spade and two boxes of stuff from the shed.

A cheerful man in a red cardigan was sitting out front, showing people where to put things. Lizzie carried all the items from the back of the car to the miscellaneous objects area. The axe and the spade had been cleaned. She left them among the garden tools, and the various items of electrical equipment and dusty old antiques. She stood the spade up at the back, behind an old lawn-mower and leaning up against the giant steel wall of the bottle bank. She put the axe beside it and she walked away from these things, and over towards where the glass bottles and old picture frames were. In her younger years she would have lingered here, and looked at the cracked pictures, the ancient sewing machines and type-writers. She would have tried to get something for herself from among all this junk, and take it home.

"Help yourself," said the man in the cardigan. He came so close that Lizzie could smell his rancid breath. "Take whatever you like, love."

"Thanks," said Lizzie. "But I don't need anything else. I'm clearing out. I'm moving away."

"Somewhere nice?"

"Hope so," she said; and she gave the man a flat-handed wave and said she'd probably be back the next day with more junk. "My husband was a sculptor," she said, not to him but to herself, as she got back into the car.

Tom

When I go back to that house and roam around it in my mind, I see her sitting out by the shed on a Sunday afternoon with her trainers crossed at the end of her spindly long legs. I see her with her head thrown back against the shed wall and her eyes closed in the sun. She is peaceful. "Aren't we lucky?" she says. She sniffs the air. I sit beside her and smile.

She asks how long I think my grandfather has left to live. I don't answer her. It doesn't seem to matter now. I am strangely happy. We like each other, we make each other laugh.

"Have you seen the flowers, Tom?"

"It's a lovely garden. So green under the trees."

"I think we're very lucky," she says, and I can sense an urgency, a kind of protest in her voice. "I didn't used to be like this. I didn't used to feel this way about life. It doesn't matter what happened or didn't. Or what went wrong. Things were and they weren't. I can't compare it to anything."

I close my eyes and tilt my face into the sun. As I've said before, I tell her, she can say what she likes about herself. I'm not interested in the stories.

"I think a shrink would be," she says bluntly.

I shrug. "Great!" I say, and then I grin, and get up to go for a run.

The freezer men come, and the lorry makes it under the branches in the lane. It is a Saturday afternoon and I am there for her. Up above, the branches scrape and scratch as it comes down the lane. Lizzie has been bending down inside the freezer all morning with hot water and the green rubber gardening gloves. I don't bother to ask why. But I feel that she needs something from me when the men come into the house and walk through the kitchen to the garage. I feel the heaviness when I am standing beside her. That little thing inside again trying to jump out and tug on my sleeve. I make a joke that the men don't get. It doesn't matter. Lizzie laughs. We laugh at each other, at ourselves. I'm a Funny One, she's a Funny One.

We look like tramps. And when the freezer is finally lifted into the back of the lorry, we are standing together in the lane in old loose clothes, and she takes a deep breath.

"It's just a feeling," I tell her. "It'll go." We lock the house up. We take Rita with us and go for a walk in the woods.

I see her waking up in a summery shirt and cotton trousers. She stands with that nest of hair on her head and lifts her arms up to the ceiling. She stands for a long time at the windows watching the woods. She asks about my grandfather. She wants to talk about the sign he taped to her car. She wants to know who he is, where he came from.

We are often looking out of the windows, or sitting in the garden looking at the trees. We are waiting for something to happen.

I bring a radio. It goes on with the news, and then it goes off again. She wanders around and sniffs things. I find it funny. I sniff with her. I wonder what she is looking for. I've heard about the five stages of grief at the end of a relationship. I start to see that she is moving between them, drifting back and forth, and trying to move on.

"Do you want to learn how to cook, Tom?"

"Will you teach me?"

She goes into the garden, to the sparkling spring morning, and picks a bunch of daffodils. She puts them in water on the sill in the kitchen. Then she opens the drawer with the knives in it.

"Probably best to have five knives to start with. And a good steel for sharpening. The vegetable knife needs to be razor sharp—keep it for carrots, onions, garlic, leeks. Then a medium-sized knife, a filleter, for trimming meat and fish, and a large one for cutting up meat and poultry. I like a long, thin-bladed ham knife for cold meat and anything that needs to be thinly sliced. Then a bread knife. But try to keep it for bread only."

I sit at the kitchen table and listen to her. I have enough money to buy a good set of knives. I know where to get them.

"I can manage fine," I say.

"I know that," she snaps back.

"And I know that I have to make a life for myself. I know you're trying to help me move on."

"I'm not trying anything of the sort. Who am I to help anyone?"

"Well, you are," I say. "You just are."

I go up to see my family at the farm.

I think they are going to ask me what I am doing there. They don't ask. Everyone is tired, and trying to get on, get by. Nic is on her way back. Mike has moved in. He's waiting for her. She calls and throws him off. He makes her laugh, and waits. My mother sits at the kitchen table drinking white wine. Erik's out shouting at the cows. Claire says she's fine. And Grandfather's fine. He wants to come for a visit, she says. There's nothing to see, I tell her. "There's nothing there."

When I get back, Lizzie has her yellow apron on. She is busy washing potatoes in the sink. She wants to talk more about the things I'm going to need.

"I'd get a clock for the kitchen, Tom. Once you've

cleaned everything out and painted the walls. We'll assume you're starting from scratch, and the room has nothing in it but oven with hob, fridge, freezer, cupboards, work surfaces, sink. Modern ovens have built-in timers, but a wall clock, or a small one for the windowsill or the sideboard."

"I'm not taking notes now, Lizzie," I say. But she doesn't seem to hear me. She keeps scrubbing away at the sink in her apron and staring out of the window at the garden while she speaks.

"Who doesn't love the peace of their own kitchen, Tom? There's something so special about it, isn't there? After all that noise and activity during the day. To just come in at night and find it still, and the floor cold, and the clock ticking away.

"When I'm cooking, I try to think that the person I'm cooking for is a little sad. Not especially hungry, not to the point where food is simply matter that must be ingested at once, but someone who might have temporarily lost their sense of taste, someone in mourning, perhaps, or sad for no particular reason, detached from themselves by worry or doubt, and trying their best to press on regardless. Imagine him, or her—hangdog, and old-feeling—and imagine yourself very carefully trying to liven them, have them blinking in gentle disbelief at the small pot of mayonnaise and prawns that you have set down before them at two o'clock on a bleak Sunday afternoon. Picture this person, and their need for summer pudding, perhaps, and hold him or her in your mind, while you crack, and mix and stir. Take it slowly, do it with the utmost care. And have a little faith. You can do this, Tom. Say it again: mayonnaise won't be made at all if you begin with the thought that it is going to separate."

She doesn't talk about Jacob. I don't ask. I think: she is making the best of this. One day they will get a divorce.

"I'd get a good pair of scales, Tom. A measuring jug, palette knife, perforated slicer, pepper and salt mill, three wooden spoons of varying sizes, a spatula, a pair of kitchen scissors, a small sieve, a colander. I'd get these things first, Tom, before you do anything else. And an apron, if you fancy it; several tea towels, a dishcloth, scourer, washing-up liquid and brush. As for boards, I like to have a wooden chopping board, about twelve by eighteen inches; a board for slicing and serving bread and cheese, and a smaller plastic board for garlic and onions. I'd buy a couple of mixing bowls, glass or plastic, and also some airtight boxes for storing vegetables, salads and fresh herbs in the fridge. I like to keep a couple of muslin squares for draining cheese or straining fruits, plus a plate rack for saucepan lids, some ovenproof plates and serving dishes, glass jars for storing rice, pasta, flour, sugar, coffee, et cetera; tin foil, greaseproof paper, cling film."

We walk in the woods together. Lizzie rides my bike.

She climbs onto it and is like a child, laughing. She takes it up to work on her first morning.

Joanna writes a letter. She hasn't been able to get through on email. Lizzie took the laptop to the dump. Lizzie picks the post up from the mat when we get back from work. It is a short, handwritten letter. Joanna wants to come and look at the figurines. Lizzie goes to stand in the garden in her coat.

I follow her out. I ask her how her day at work was. She doesn't answer. I go back inside. She follows me and asks if I will drive the sculptures to London for her. I ask why the woman can't come to collect them.

"Because, Tom," she flashes back, and then stands there, eyes blazing, lips pinched. I can see the anger. She doesn't know what to do with it. She is trying to smile.

"If you're angry," I say, "then for fuck's sake just be angry."

"Yes," she says, and goes upstairs.

"How do you know she'll like them?" I ask the following morning when we are packing them into a box for me to take to the car.

"She thinks he was good. I didn't."

"How can you say these are rubbish?" I ask her, holding one of the little leaping boys in my hand. I wrap it in pages of the local newspaper.

"I don't."

"They're so delicate. So beautiful."

"Yes," she says. "There's something innocent about them."

"I guess it takes an artist to know another."

"I'm not an artist. I never was."

"Were you scared?"

"Scared of what?" she says.

"Of him? Of his talent. What he could do."

Lizzie had been in a car crash at the age of twelve.

Life went on. People died. The sea roared. Dogs ran around and barked.

"You pay your bills and you go to work," she said, getting in the car one morning, and showing me a bit of leg under her skirt.

I didn't know. I had no idea. I was with a woman twice my age. I could see that it was possible to wake up every morning and feel happy.

I could see that it was possible to wake up.

"Tom! It's morning!"

Like a child. "It's morning."

She was trying to start again.

"Children are playful, trusting, happy and alive, Tom."

Children are bounding up the stairs with the sun.

She tells me about her mother. I picture a tall, independent woman striding along a beach.

Boom, she says, in a way that suggests death bookends everything, curtailing her experience over and over again. She mentions her father once, says he was from Ireland, and that was all she knew. All she would ever know. There wasn't anything else.

It turns out that we both hated being alone. I was lonely and she was lonely. It didn't matter much what we did when we were together. Just that we were, in that short time as much as we could be, together.

How could love ever have been a calm, gentle gut feeling like a big growing peony or a happy rock down there? For Lizzie it was an intermittent stabbing sensation in the heart and lung area so that a desire to give was always associated unconsciously with a slight inability to breathe. And love came with a sense of loss. All she had lost. That had made her work terribly hard.

"You need what we all need, Tom," she says. "You need what we all need."

Which is love. And the peace of mind to feel it.

"That's part of the problem," she says. "You can feel love, and know that you love someone deeply. But in your mind you're going to be quietly unraveling it. So that comfort doesn't come. Because how could you bear it? To latch on, and be pushed away, with your mouth open and your hands flailing madly?"

Lizzie had found a person willing to learn from her. I'd found someone I could "be" around. I was fascinated. I didn't ask questions.

"You're so laid-back, Tom," she says.

Then I tell her that my grandfather wants to visit. She

goes quiet. After a while she says it's not possible. No one can come.

On Saturday morning at the end of our week Lizzie comes to the garden center and she walks around with her head tucked down on her neck. From time to time she looks over at me. She has her hair behind her ears. She comes to the checkout with a jasmine to plant down by the wall. She wants something to grow up the south-facing side of the shed.

We have an argument about my grandfather coming to visit. I say, "He only wants to pop in! Can't we give anyone a cup of tea?"

I know that the time is coming for me to go.

15

Lizzie left a note. With instructions for the dog. She left the house keys under the mat. She took the cool bag and she put Jacob's head inside it. She had removed it from its bin liner and wrapped it in fifteen sheets of newspaper. There were four ice blocks inside it, and she would stop for bags of ice on the way. She kissed and ruffled and left the dog.

She rang Bob and said that she hadn't made a decision about the car after all. She was going to leave it at home for now. There were four legs of the journey: a cab to Guildford, train to London Waterloo, across London on the Underground, then up to Scotland.

She got into the taxi with the black holdall that had been at the top of the stairs for seventeen days, and the cool bag. She put the holdall in the boot and sat with the cool bag on the seat beside her.

As the taxi turned around and then bumped up the lane, she kept her arm resting on the bag, and her chin tilted up in the back window.

🍴

212. When the train arrives on Platform 3 at Guildford station and the doors open, go inside and find yourself a seat. You will see that there is a luggage compartment in which you can store your bags.

213. Put the holdall down first and then the cool bag on top of it.

214. Resist the urge to stand nervously guarding your bags.

215. When the coffee cart comes round, order yourself a coffee.

216. You need do nothing else. You have the essentials in your handbag. Simply sit and sip the coffee. Take in the view.

217. You will arrive at Waterloo forty-seven minutes after the train has left Guildford.

218. Your train from Euston doesn't leave until four in the afternoon. This gives you plenty of time to get across London on the Underground (take the Northern Line, seven stops) and find a place to buy ice.

219. When you get to Euston, check your holdall into a locker. You will find them close to the toilets. Collect your ticket from a machine using the card you used to purchase online.

220. Look up at the boards and make a mental note of your platform. Usually the Glasgow train leaves from Platform 9.

221. Once you've noted the platform number, take the
cool bag with you out through the main entrance.
Turn left outside and walk towards a small parade
of shops. There is a newsagent there with three
small freezers in the middle of the shop. Here you
will find ice. Buy one bag and ask for a plastic bag
to carry it in. You might need two plastic bags.
222. Go back to the station and walk towards the toilets.
You will need 30p to use the facilities. Once inside
a cubicle, lay the bags of ice carefully around the
head. Check the old ice blocks to see if they have
thawed. If so, leave them in the cubicle.

In her dreams, they had all come to help her; to take over
the last bits, the cleaning up. In reality, Tom hadn't come
back to help her with the shed as he'd said he might,
and Joanna hadn't come down in her zippy little car
and bounced up the steps to help her either. They'd not
found the three beautiful figurines of a boy—leaping,
reading, and standing laughing with his hands in his
pockets—and they'd not laid them out on the garden table and had a little cry over the wasted years. Joanna
hadn't taken them away in her zippy little car, and Tom
hadn't held Lizzie's hand and promised to turf the lawn
and take care of the dog and the house and the garden.
No one had come, and the silence had clung and oppressed her, reminding her through the cleaning, the
sweeping, the closing of doors to each room behind her

that we all have to look after ourselves, and things can't be rushed, and we can't start again.

Except that Lizzie felt she owed it to herself to try.

❡

223. You may not feel like eating, but try to have something. Even a bit of cake from the café you go to to get your coffee in its takeaway cup.

224. You are starting to feel that you are part of the world. You see yourself standing on a busy station concourse in London with a cup of coffee in your hand and a couple of bags at your feet. To people passing by you are a woman going on a trip, heading north for a weekend away. You have a little smile on your face. Now people know you are doing something that you are looking forward to.

225. You stand on the concourse and feel the crowd surge around you as you take sips of your coffee.

226. This is what it feels like to be part of the world.

227. Don't think about what's in the bag at your feet.

228. Don't worry about the ice melting or what happens next.

229. Find the platform and walk the long length of a shiny new fast train that will carry you all the way from London to Glasgow.

230. Get to carriage B, and put your holdall in the

luggage compartment. Put the cool bag there too, up high.

231. For a moment or two you think about whether you might have been able to leave it on the station concourse. How long it would take a member of the surging crowd to find it, open it, and work out what it was. Then you realize that some poor cleaner would most likely find it, and that they might not recover from the trauma. Because you don't want to hurt anyone, you take the cool bag with you and you settle on the train.

16

Lizzie looked at the gray buildings and the thick, heavy sky over London as the train pushed north through the suburbs and broke into open fields. She didn't think of the house except to ask herself if everything had been done as she'd said it would be. She'd been very busy, and being busy had kept her from herself for days. She hadn't had further thoughts about the police station or about old Emmett and his signs. The busier one was, she'd found, the easier life could be. Without thought, without feeling, one just had to have stamina. Soon, she realized, gazing out of the window, it would all be over.

So now she was giving herself the best possible chance of starting again. She would need a freezer and then she would need a job. Sitting in the warmth of the train carriage with the smell of other humans around her, she let the muscles in her neck relax and she stretched out the muscles in her hands and fingers. If she could just carry on like this—minute by minute—and not let the world crash in and startle her too much, then she might just make it and really get away.

Lizzie tried to get some sleep. She knew that the journey would take four and a half hours, and so she settled back into the seat, worked on feeling relaxed, but she felt very upright, and she was staring, wide-eyed, out of the window with both hands around her coffee cup. In her mind she tried to imagine a slim woman with clean curls and tired skin gazing out at the fields and picturing a better life. She sniffed, tried to stretch her awareness into all corners of the carriage for someone who might think her odd, or suspicious, or be able to detect something amiss in the air and atmosphere.

It was dark and late when Lizzie arrived in Glasgow. She had not slept. She had listened to her heart beating all the way there. She pushed to be first off the train, collected her bags from the luggage compartment, and began to blow loudly from her mouth, to detract attention from any smell that might have been coming from the bag as she stood in the cramped area between two carriages with other passengers. As soon as the doors opened, she stepped out onto the platform and walked hurriedly with her bags, not noticing the cold, not thinking of anything but her need to get to an all-night supermarket for some ice.

There were so many people still on the station concourse and the buildings outside the station were tall and looming in the dark. She would not be able to find a bed and settle down here, she realized; even asking someone to recommend a place to stay seemed too much. Hunkering down with her bags and trying not to get too cold was the best she would be able to do this night, and keeping his head outside felt much safer to her than trying to take it in somewhere.

So Lizzie made her way to a supermarket and she bought three new bags of ice. There would be coffee bars she could go to, to warm up, if need be; and she walked the streets with her bags on her shoulders and the plastic bag of ice in her hand feeling newly alert and alive to the challenge of finding herself here. She no longer thought to worry about what people looking in at her might see. People were busy; caught up in their own dramas, and seeing only what they wanted to see. No one in the world was looking for a cannibal in a tall woman from Puttenham and so she ducked into the first open coffee shop she came to and went at once to the toilets to recharge the ice.

At four in the morning, she sat on a bench on the concourse at Glasgow station and she watched water being sprayed on the floor from a motorized cleaning machine. The lights were still on overhead though the shops had long been closed and barred. She watched pigeons fly down from the roof and a lost dog come running in and running out again. She thought of Rita and tried to imagine her here with her, lying at her feet with one ear up, one eyebrow lifted, looking around, overwhelmed. It pierced her heart to think of the dog, her loving eyes, and warmth, and she looked around the station, trying to find something, anything to keep her eyes on. This wasn't a way to begin her future, but she lacked the energy right at the moment to think of another option. She let herself lie down on the bench, her back muscles hunched and tense against the cold. Just imagine, she told herself, that Jacob is in the garden chair; he is sitting at home, knowing I have gone. Then this new life becomes a real possibility, she thought. I have left him in order to start again. He is not my responsibility; he lives, without me, at home. It made her calmer to think of Jacob alive, being there for her, if she needed him, at home. It wasn't possible, after all, to cut bits of one's life out and go on alone as if the past had never happened. In her mind, and in her physical reality, Jacob Prain, the man she'd married, was still with her. Moving on without him was going to lead her to make a bad decision. How could she trust her own judgment? He would have to be included, she felt, in all that she set out to do.

Lizzie uncurled her legs, and got up from the bench. There was still an ache in her stomach from the consumption at the weekend of all that had been left, and she was feeling weary now from the journey, and the final cleaning frenzy she had put herself through.

The youth hostel was a ten-minute walk from the station, and by the time she arrived she was feeling very cold. It was six o'clock in the morning, and the hostel wasn't open yet. Lizzie sat outside, on her bag. Her coat and scarf weren't nearly thick enough for the Scottish weather, but until she found a job and could buy something else, perhaps from a charity shop, they would have to do. She hadn't much money and the train ticket and ice supplies, the coffee and food had eaten up one hundred pounds. She would have to take it slowly from here, cut the coffee out, drink tap water, think ahead and write everything down.

232. You are starting to get very tired.
233. Find somewhere to rest.
234. You've gone without sleep now for forty-eight hours and you've not slept properly since the beginning of March.
235. There will be a youth hostel where you can find a bed. There may well be a deep freeze in the kitchen at the hostel. You could say that you have been staying on a cattle farm and have bought some meat that you would like to keep frozen.
236. Book yourself a room for the day and for the night.
237. Anyone looking in will see only a bag of ice on top and a layer of newspaper underneath.

At the hostel, Lizzie lay down on the clean sheets of the lower bunk and let her body sink into the mattress. She slept for five and a half hours, and when she woke, she decided to venture out in search of somewhere to eat. She took the cool bag with her and found a place down a cobbled street where they said it would be all right if she sat outside, at one of the metal tables on the street. The patron, who was wearing a bow tie, explained that he had no patio heaters and she might get very cold. Lizzie smiled and said that was fine. Then she asked him for a glass of red wine and a bowl of whatever soup he had. She had a cigarette and she read through the menu, just to see what was on it and because she could; then she sat back in her chair, with Jacob's head underneath it, and she watched the street and the people walking and she tried to figure out from their faces and footsteps what sort of lives they might be leading.

"Lizzie, I think that between us, we do have the imagination to make this work, to make a success of our cakes."

"It isn't about imagination, Jacob, but application, hard work, and making sure that enough people out there know what we're trying to do."

"I disagree," he'd said, and shook his head, though he hadn't been able to add anything else.

"Jacob?"

"Yes?"

"Do you still love me?"

"For goodness sake!"

"Do you think you ever did?"

Tom

Even after years, and with a new life, I am still that boy at the garden center biking back to the house in the woods. I come back to a shiny hatchback parked in the lane, and I find that Joanna is there, standing out in the garden with Lizzie. I see the two of them as I step through the kitchen and I know it's her, that shock of white hair, and I can tell from the body language that something is wrong. Lizzie is standing back on her heels with her arms folded; Joanna also has her arms folded, shielding her body, and one hand is pressed flat against the side of her nodding face. It looks as if the visitor is being told something she doesn't believe. It looks as if she isn't going until she has got what she came for.

I breeze out. "Afternoon all," I say, and I feel my chest puffing up, my shoulders rising to the challenge this woman from London has brought to our hidey-hole in the woods. Suddenly I hate the hatchback, and the scruffy jeans and the bangles the woman is wearing over the sleeves of a long gray cardigan. Beside Joanna Lizzie looks like a stiff, startled giraffe. Her clothes and hair look cheap and faded.

I hear her say, "Oh God, I'm *fine!*" then she sees me

and claps her hands in front of her breasts and calls me over, rubbing her hands together like a nervous person preparing for a speech.

I go feeling heavy and sick and faint in case somehow this woman is going to bring an end to the happiness here, or make some remark, or show me a face that tells me she doesn't approve of my being here.

"This is Tom," says Lizzie, loudly.

"Yes," says Joanna. "He came to see me in London."

The corners of Joanna's mouth push out to the sides in a flat fixed smile.

"I just know that Jacob would reply to me," she says. "I believed in him. I know that he wouldn't take off like that. I just think that... Oh, I don't know. I feel like I'm not getting the whole picture here. I'm sorry for just arriving, but I felt that we had to talk."

Lizzie is smiling in a sweet and friendly way with her head tipping way down to the side. Her face seems to be reflecting the green from the trees. Her chin is stiff as flint.

"Can I get you anything?" I ask the air between them and then look from one to the other.

Joanna sighs and splits the straps of her handbag along her cashmered arm to fish around in the contents for her keys,

"No," she says, shaking her head into her bag. The voice that has been politely controlled behind a trembling lip and an arch, slightly pleading way of speaking—trying to have a discussion rather than an ar-gument—gives way now to a series of whimpers as she looks at each of us in turn and says she'll be in touch soon.

Lizzie walks into the kitchen in long manly strides and pours herself a glass of white wine from the bottle in the fridge.

"My grandfather wants to come and see us," I say. "And Mike and Nic. They just want to pop in and see."

"See what?"

"Us! Me. Here!"

Her knees go. She sinks into a chair at the table and rests her head on the wood.

"You have to leave now, Tom."

"What?"

"You should go. It's been very pleasant having you here, but really, now, that's enough."

I sit down at the table.

"I don't want to go, though. We're fine here."

"You have to find a home of your own now," she says. "Not hang around here, clinging on to me."

"Who's the one clinging on?"

She drains her glass, and stands up. A blast of cold air whips around the room as the back door swings open.

"I can't go," I tell her. "I don't know where to go."

"You'll find somewhere quite quickly," she says, turn-ing now in the doorway to the kitchen and folding her arms. She is looking upwards, as if calculating how long it will take her to get her rucksack out from under the bed and make her move.

I laugh, sit back in my chair like a boy waiting for punches. "We are cool!"

"Don't be ridiculous."

I laugh. I don't know what else to do.

"Fuck it," I say. "I'll go home. If you don't want me here!"

"I do," she says, softening, turning back into the room. "I do want you here. But we need to make sure that no one else comes here, Tom. We need to know that Joanna won't come to find us, that no one will. It'll just be us, Tom. That's the way it has to be. Do you understand?"

She stands there smiling at me. Through her tears she is bright red, and her mouth is forming into a tiny circle through which it seems she is trying to suck some air in.

"It has to be just us if you stay here, Tom. Because I've done something…"

17

"Could you sell me some ice?" Lizzie said to the waitress when she came to clear her bowl and plate. The waitress frowned and wrinkled her nose while clearing the table, pushing her nostrils out, as if she had smelled something foul. She said they didn't sell ice.

Lizzie felt herself going very red. After the waitress had gone she sniffed under her chair. There was something there. It was indistinct. She put her head further down and sniffed again. Then she withdrew her head and looked around at the street. She went back under and sniffed again; pulled her head back up, took in some air. She glugged back the rest of her wine. It was hard to know what was worse: being down there with it and fully aware of how the smell was developing, or being up above the table where the smell was so faint she couldn't keep tabs on it.

She had thought there would be more time before he woke up. She had thought she would get the night to sleep a little with it out on the windowsill at least. She had hoped to be able to find a little studio flat in the morning, with a freezer. Even one that came above or below a fridge. She would have been able to take the shelf out and squeeze the head right in.

"Not so," she whispered tightly.

She left the cool bag under the table and went into the restaurant to pay for her soup. She walked towards the counter hoping to avoid contact with the waitress, who was down the back of the room, standing beside the door to the toilets pinning up her hair. She caught Lizzie's eye in the mirror and didn't smile.

Lizzie fumbled in her bag for her purse and pulled out a twenty-pound note to pay for her meal.

She lit a cigarette just as soon as she was out and decided to smoke at all times while carrying the bag. Wherever she went from now on, she would walk in a cloud of cigarette smoke so that no one could get near her and smell what was in the bag she was carrying.

She turned left at the end of the street and walked in the direction of the all-night supermarket. If she got three more bags of ice, and replenished tonight, she would surely be able to leave the bag on the windowsill and get a night's sleep.

She loosened the strap on the cool bag so that she could put it over one arm and over her head and drape it diagonally across her body. She now had it square on her stomach, which meant that she could put her arms around it, and blow smoke directly onto the blue material. She had bought a bag with wipe-clean foil lining, and Endura thermal insulation, but it wasn't working as it should.

"You had to bloody wake up," she whispered to the bag as she walked along. "You couldn't let me be."

At least she wasn't home now. At least she'd got away from the woods. She stood on the street, in the dark, and lit another cigarette. When a large burly man staggered towards her muttering to himself, she blew smoke in a downward plume so that it would billow around the bag and then drift upwards around her. A vision of Jacob's head, then his corduroy trousers, came into her mind. She blew more smoke out and flapped her hand around the bag.

She dared not leave the bag outside the all-night supermarket, but went in with it for ice, and deodorant, which she sprayed there and then, all over herself, while pretending to experience the scent in the aisle. She chose a man's deodorant, believing it to be stronger—it was the one Jacob had used—and she sprayed this around her feet as she walked towards the counter to pay. She also bought a bottle of disinfectant and some chewing gum for her breath.

There was one other person booked into her room, and the girl was asleep under a mass of black hair. Lizzie gasped when she switched her bedside light on and saw the tattooed roses wrapped around the girl's upper arm. It was freezing cold out, so the head went on the sill, and Lizzie opened her holdall, got changed into her nightclothes, and slipped under the duvet. For a long time she lay there, stiff on her back, and holding the covers in her hands. Her eyes were fixed open on the slats of the bed above.

She did sleep, and when she woke she had the sensation, for the first time in weeks, of having been gently lifted out of a peaceful dream. For a brief moment she felt as if she were starting again, like a child. Then the thought of what was on the sill and all she would have to do today crowded in on her, and she shut her eyes before fully registering the air coming in through the open window.

The bag was gone.

Lizzie got up very quickly and pulled her clothes on. Her heart was beating very fast and her hands were shaking.

"I found it," said the huge Glaswegian woman sitting at the counter.

"Could I have it?" Lizzie asked. She could feel the sweat running down her sides.

"Why would you leave your things outside?"

"I…I just put it on the sill to keep it cool. It's a *cool bag!*" said Lizzie, and her voice was very high.

"I can see that!" said the woman as she pulled her knitted cardigan in over her breasts. With one of her eyes she was looking at the air to the left of Lizzie's head.

"Where is it?" Lizzie asked.

"It's right here. At my feet."

"Can I have it, please?"

"Course," said the woman, and she pushed her chair back and bent forward. Lizzie dashed round behind the counter and leaped for the bag.

"Urgh!" cried the woman, as Lizzie pushed to the side under the desk. She heaved herself back in the chair. "What the bloody...!"

"I'm so sorry," Lizzie spluttered on her knees. She grabbed the bag with both hands and dragged it past the woman's legs. The smell was unbearable. "I'm so sorry. I'm going. I'm leaving. I'm going to get right out of your way now."

The woman was staring at her with her mouth open.

"It's not gone six a.m.!" she said, as if it was hard for her to believe there could be this much nervous energy in another human being. "What's the name?" she said, with one eyebrow raised.

"I'm Lizzie," came the reply as Lizzie ran back around the counter.

"Lizzie who?"

"Prain," said Lizzie, and then she turned in the corridor and tried to sling the stinking cool bag over her shoulder as she walked, striding manfully away.

Tom

In my mind, I go back and it's like the last time.

I am cycling fast in a thick fog in the dark. I swerve onto the verge above the cycle path, sit back on the bike and release the handlebar. The bike skates down the hill towards a valley.

I push hard, head down, past damp thatched cottages in the village, past the primary school, past the post office, and a steamed-up mirror on the bend. Past the Dog and Duck with the climbing frame in the garden, a horse lifting its head by a fence, a trough with twigs frozen in the ice, and water on the field, a dip and a mud-caked road.

I spin at the turning for Tubford Lane, and I am in the woods. Alder trees with skinny catkins. I bike past the faded blue Volvo, and come to a dark, stifled house on the bend.

I know her story now. I have known it for twenty-four hours. During that time I have not slept. I have been to work and tripped around.

I throw the bike at the yew hedge and stumble on the stone steps, through an unlocked door, not stopping to stretch or breathe, or take the helmet off. I am in my cycling gear. I switch the lights on to signs of life having moved on. I see a note on the kitchen table. And an envelope with a letter inside it.

She'd left the hostel straightaway that morning and got on a train from Glasgow.

Once she was on the train, there was nothing to do but sit there hoping.

"I just had to sit and hope," she says, "that people would tolerate it, not feel so oppressed that they would be forced to make inquiries or a complaint to the ticket inspector.

"Every time he came to check my ticket," she says, "I thought it was going to be time. I sat there watching him wrinkle his nose; and I could see that the carriage I was in was virtually empty. People had had to evacuate the carriage. I didn't blame them. So sinister," she says. "A smell like that. The way it creeps up on you and stops your heart."

I am exhausted.

"I can't imagine your being able to stay here now that you know."

I have nothing to say.

We sit in silence.

I go into the kitchen to try to make a cup of tea. It has come like a bomb in the night, ripping the nipple out of the mouth.

I am flailing, in panic. Tomorrow I will go to work.

I make the tea and stare at it. She is quiet.

"I didn't know what to do with the body," she says. "I remembered something someone had said at work once. About how if it came to it, and she found herself with a dead body in her house and had to get rid of it in order to not get caught, she would most likely—"

"From something someone said at work?"

"Yes," she says. Her hands are shaking around her teacup.

"What would you like me to do, Tom?"

"What would I like you to do?"

"What shall I do?"

We stand in the kitchen together. I drink from the cup and try to think about something else.

I turn my face towards the garden and think of the lawn, how emerald green it is in spring with the light coming through the trees.

It doesn't have to have anything to do with me.

"I don't expect you to stay here, Tom. I'm so grateful for what we've had."

Lizzie opens up her handbag. I think for a moment that she is about to get her checkbook out and write me a check. I close my eyes. I try to breathe.

*   *   *

"Talk to me, Tom?" she says, in a small, trembling voice.

"I had a girlfriend at university," I say.

I look up at Lizzie. I feel it is important to carry on talking, to try and keep saying something.

Funny how all that stuff about being in the moment falls away.

She is holding on to the sideboard and she has gone very pale.

I try to imagine what she did with his feet.

"I did not know what else to do," she says.

"You should have turned yourself in."

"I did not want to."

"You what?"

"I did not want to, Tom. I want to live. I want to have a life!"

I'm not sure I have fully taken in what she has said.

Denial. Then anger. She says that she had the same reaction. That he was in the freezer for days.

Now I understand the worry about the freezer men coming in the lorry to take it away.

I cannot imagine how a person is able to eat another person's hand. Happily, I do not have that imagination.

I know instantly, and I understand, what has driven her to do it. I just can't imagine how. I can't believe it possible for a human being to endure having to live through that—the days of waking and knowing and cutting and forcing it down.

What could I do? she says.

"You should have turned yourself in. You need to."

I keep looking out at the trees. It is dark, but they are out there. I remember how we have both been standing looking out at the trees. Trying to find a path in the woods. I can't bear to be near here.

"Yes, of course," she says.

"It's not love, Lizzie."

"What, Tom? What isn't?"

"Why did nothing stop you? It's love that stops a person from doing that. Where is the love that should have come and stopped you? Where is love, Lizzie?"

"Nothing could stop me," she says. "Once I'd made the decision."

I say it again: "Where is love?"

I would have to go. It gave us something to fight against. It made us stretch out what we had as far as it would go. I wondered how I could leave her. I thought back to the beginning. Simple things: cups of coffee, morning walks, watching the rain on the window. When the end is inevitable and coming that fast. She must always have known that the end was coming. She would always have had a moment in her mind when she would tell me. What I couldn't understand was how quickly I absorbed the knowledge that Lizzie

Prain was not the sort of woman who could turn herself in. She hadn't gone to the police. She had been too frightened, too determined. She had been in flight from the moment she killed him.

She had taken the hand in her own hands and rubbed it all over with olive oil and salt. She had laid it in a roasting tray and put it in the oven. Onto the top shelf. A clean tea towel to take it out, to hold it in her hands. She had put his fingers in her mouth.

These are the things I can't think about.

Or the blow from the axe that pulled his body apart from his head.

"We only see what we want to see, Tom."

She called me Funny One Tom.

"Don't say that. Please!"

I didn't have the words. I was saying things I'd heard from other people.

"How do we manage to live, Tom?"

She turned her head to look at me and I saw how small and dark her eyes had become. I saw the lines on her face, pinched around her mouth. I had loved the ray of sun in her, the constant waking up and saying what a wonderful day, how wonderful it was to be alive.

"You can never tell another person, Tom."

I, who had never been interested in the stories anyone told me about themselves.

247

*　*　*

She was useless. I was useless. Ripples of disgust for both of us ran through me.

I had thought him abroad. With someone younger than Lizzie. I had thought that he had gone after thirty years of marriage to start again.

"I won't tell anyone."

I wasn't going to imagine more than I needed to.

"Did you manage to get through it all, Lizzie?"

"All of it," she said, and looked away.

The day after she told me, I came home from work and I found her note.

Please take the letter in the envelope with you, Tom. I've gone to spend the night at the Cornstack in Elstead. Rita is with me. We'll go to work at the hotel tomorrow. When we get back I'd really like you to have gone. Thank you so much for everything. Please, don't look for me again.

18

At the Cornstack in Elstead, lying in a single bed with her hands folded on her stomach, Lizzie remembered her pictures, the partridge photographs she'd pinned up on the walls of the shed in her twenties. She'd sat in there, in the shed, with all the tools around her, and she'd been pleased with the photographs. Then she'd wondered what on earth she was doing with her time. Jacob had liked the pictures. He'd said it was fine to sit in a woodland shed looking at photographs of woods. "What's the problem with that?" he'd said. So then she'd carried on a bit, taking pictures after dark, and there had been one photograph of hers that he'd liked. She'd always had a torch in the lane, because night and day, from where the trees had reached across above and grabbed each other, there had been no light and what had felt like very little air.

Lizzie looked at her watch. She knew that Tom would have returned from work by now. He wouldn't be there in the morning when she and Rita went back in the car, and she didn't think he'd go back to the farm. There was nothing further that she could do. Telling him had been an accident, and yet entirely necessary: without it he might never have gone; they would have clung to each other for a decade.

Lizzie breathed and looked up at the ceiling. She remembered the anxiety she'd felt coming back from Scotland, running through the house with the awful cool bag to whip the head out and run with it down to the bottom of the garden where she'd tried to tuck it down in the hole but hadn't had enough room. In a panic, in the dark, she'd used her hands to lift up earth from the flower bed, and she'd kept it in there, and the dog inside, overnight. All day it had taken her to make that hole big enough to take his head, and the clods of earth, then the tree. All day she had feared Tom coming back from work early, or Emmett arriving, coming through the gate at the bottom, crawling mad and decrepit, with mud on his face, under the yew hedge to find her digging, Jacob's head beside her, stinking, rotting, waiting to go in.

Lizzie placed her hands on her stomach, and breathed in. She had passed the saloon car as she'd driven away in the Volvo. Erik had been driving, one of his thin daughters staring out of the window in the back. Lizzie hadn't been able to tell which one of the twins it was, but she wondered now if it was Nic coming back from the station. Emmett hadn't been in the car. In the quick glance, she'd looked for him. She felt she would always, in a split-second glance, be looking for him.

In her head there was a sense of quickening, what felt

like an idea. She liked it here. At the desk downstairs was the same man who'd seen her last time when she'd tried to leave her husband and then gone back again. She had apologized about leaving so early.

"I've left something at home," she'd said, and crept on out to the car. Then she'd driven back to Puttenham, out past the Dog and Duck, past the climbing frame in the field, and the horse holding its head—half up half down—by the fence, left into Tubford Lane, then bumpety bump bump to the house.

She'd parked the Volvo in the lane, walked into the kitchen and put the apron on as if she'd been there all night, sleeping beside her husband, or folded downstairs on the sofa with the dog. Radio on, cookery book in its customary place, dog stretching on its bed, and yawning with a yelp to see her coming back in.

Jacob had been talking about planting some trees. Alder grew well in dark places. It grew to ninety feet. She'd read, in the *Farnham Herald,* that the catkins of some alders, like the red alder in America, for example, were rich in protein, and though they had a bitter flavor, they were included on the "plants of the future" website, and could be eaten, in extremis, for survival. She'd wanted to tell him that. She'd opened her mouth to speak about it, but he was already leaving the room.

Oak, he'd said. He'd wanted some booming trees that would one day grow big enough to undermine the wall.

He'd known, she was sure of it, that she'd tried to

leave him. He'd known that she'd failed. He hadn't been smug. He'd been desperate too, and hanging on.

"I'll find more work for us," he'd said, taking another roll from the baking tray, though it wasn't clear what he was going to do. He'd been thinking that they might start taking orders for bread. "Something gooey like the cakes women in Guildford have in cafés in the afternoons," he'd said, doing an impression of them pressing forkfuls of sweet creamy dough into their mouths.

"I'll go out," she'd said.

He'd been holding on to the back of the kitchen chair, smiling, embarrassed, and smiling through that; his eyes working full tilt to convey the awkwardness and pain. That had been the way to get to her. She'd never seen the effort, only the difficulty he'd been having with his feelings and whether he should say something at all. So then she'd rush in, try to help. She'd smile—why spoil it?—and let him know it was all right. They wouldn't need to talk. She had loved him—she had—with empathy and with, she thought, imagination.

They would do away with nonsense about the marriage, then. There was work to be done. Surely, somewhere, there was work to be done! And so she'd got back in the Volvo, and reversed up the lane. It had been hot still. No rain. Nothing for a week or so. And she'd been feeling this giddiness, like a high from having been away for one night at the Cornstack, and she'd driven very fast, ramming the old thing to full tilt on the motorway to get to the garden center.

She had tried to leave. But she'd gone back. Then they'd got hemmed in again by the clinging trees and the world outside and all their fear. Their fear of what was out there and of being alone had kept them going round and round in circles for thirty years.

"We don't have to be afraid!" she said to Tom before he knew.

She was sitting out by the shed, her head tilted up and back in the sun.

"No," he said and laughed.

She said: "There's not really anything to be afraid of, Tom. Not really. Not nearly as much as we think."

"Aren't we crazy to worry so much?"

He bounced up and started running on the spot, lifting his knees up to touch his chin, making his arms flap at the sides. Lizzie watched him in the sunlight, watching his smooth young skin and his hair flying and his arms moving up and down in the air as he shouted suddenly with desperation and then ran across the garden and leaped over the wall to run into the trees. She watched him go and she let her eyes close, still seeing in her mind that figure bouncing up and down in the same spot on the grass, flapping his arms, trying to lift upwards, trying to fly. Which was when it came to her, and it didn't feel like a decision; it wasn't that heavy, it didn't have weight. It was a feeling of warmth and truth and a knowledge that the way was clear now, and she was going on alone.

My name is Lizzie Prain. I am fifty-three years old. In spite of the fact that I killed and then ate my spouse, Jacob Prain, at our woodland cottage in the Surrey Hills, I have lived a good life. I have a friend who has drawn me out of myself and taught me to laugh. I have made new friends. I have enjoyed cooking, gardening, working, walking, and the company of my dog. I have an imagination but I also have a practical mind. I have not been overly troubled with or haunted by thoughts of what I did.

When I realized that my husband was dead, I also realized I had a chance to live. It was then a question of doing away with the body. Within a matter of hours, I had dismembered it, tied each segment in a heavy-duty bin liner, sealed it with a twisty, labeled it, and stored it in the deep freeze.

I have always been a good cook and someone who cares about the environment. Eating my husband was a choice, and, I like to think, a moral one.

Within a few days of achieving total consumption, I had gained weight, as had Rita, my dog. I had also got a haircut. I had been offered a job. Nothing of Jacob went to waste.

Tom Vickory is a good man. He had no part in any of

this. It was I who killed, and I who ate. I did it alone, in my kitchen and also in my garden.

Having decided I would not be found out and punished, I made the choice to live, and to live fully with the knowledge that each day after Jacob's death was a privilege. I'm no longer afraid of being discovered because I know that if I am, the bliss of my hours, my days, months and years since this unfortunate time will have made my captivity worthwhile.

This last month, I have had something to do, and I have had love. I am very lucky. It has been perfect.

Thank you.

Lizzie slept well at the Cornstack with the dog curled huge and heavy at the foot of the bed. When she woke in the morning, she had a shower and dressed in a clean shirt and jeans. The man at the desk was there again with his cup of coffee and he stood up to go and make her breakfast.

"Yogurt and fruit is absolutely fine for me," said Lizzie, and she went into the dining room with a newspaper in her hand and Rita waited for her outside the door.

It was a gray morning, and a very gentle rain was falling on the village green.

"Not dashing off quite so early this time," said the man from the desk when he brought her a pot of tea and poured it slowly into a cup for her.

Lizzie was surprised that he remembered her from time to time. She had been in such a panic, such a hurry back then. Everything nice and good and warm in her had been folded in and hidden from the world.

"Not dashing off today," she said, spreading her napkin on her lap. "Though I will be leaving shortly," she added, and then she looked at her watch, reached for her cup of tea and smiled at him.

Acknowledgments

Thank you to:
Claire Baldwin, Tassy Barham, Rebecca Carter, Jackie
Coventry, Tobi Coventry, Frances Doyle, Alex Elam, Will
Francis, Myrto Gelati, Sean Green, Mary-Anne
Harrington, Mercy Hooper, Betty Kamara, Emily
Kitchin, Jo Liddiard, Miranda Marchese, Andrea Mason,
Peter Sandison, Sacha Tanyar, Laura Tisdel, Melissa
Werndle, and Ben Willis

About the Author

Natalie Young is a London-based writer and journalist. She has written articles for *The Times*, the *Sunday Times*, *Prospect*, and *Mslexia*. More details can be found on her website: natalieyoung.co.uk.